**"It's true," Tate insisted. "Your first shift will hurt, but I guarantee it won't be like the pain of the Turn.** Your body is primed for this now. And once you've gotten it down, shifting won't hurt. Honestly, I think a lot of the pain wolflings experience with their first dozen or so shifts is psychological. It *should* hurt. Your bones and muscles are breaking and knitting themselves back together in a new configuration. Everything we know about our bodies says that should be agonizing."

Adrian huffed. "It should hurt, so it does?" He flexed his shoulders, trying to ease the crick in his neck. "Does a wolfling in a box exist as both a wolf and a human until you can open the box to prove otherwise?"

Tate brought his fingers to Adrian's neck and honed in on the knot giving him grief. Adrian went boneless at the touch.

"Schrödinger's Werewolf? I like it."

# WELCOME TO

DREAMSPUN BEYOND

Dear Reader,

Everyone knows love brings a touch of magic to your life. And the presence of paranormal thrills can make a romance that much more exciting. Dreamspun Beyond selections tell stories of love featuring your favorite shifters, vampires, wizards, and more falling in love amid paranormal twists. Stories that make your breath catch and your imagination soar.

In the pages of these imaginative love stories, readers can escape to a contemporary world flavored with a touch of the paranormal where love conquers all despite challenges, the thrill of a first kiss sweeps you away, and your heart pounds at the sight of the one you love. When you put it all together, you discover romance in its truest form, no matter what world you come from.

Love sees no difference.

*Elizabeth North*

Executive Director
Dreamspinner Press

# Bru Baker

## CAMP H.O.W.L.

PUBLISHED BY

Published by
DREAMSPINNER PRESS

5032 Capital Circle SW, Suite 2, PMB# 279,
Tallahassee, FL 32305-7886 USA
www.dreamspinnerpress.com

This is a work of fiction. Names, characters, places, and incidents either
are the product of author imagination or are used fictitiously, and any
resemblance to actual persons, living or dead, business establishments,
events, or locales is entirely coincidental.

Camp H.O.W.L.
© 2017 Bru Baker.

Cover Art
© 2017 Aaron Anderson
aaronbydesign55@gmail.com
Cover content is for illustrative purposes only and any person depicted
on the cover is a model.

ISBN: 978-1-63533-797-6
Digital ISBN: 978-1-63533-800-3
Library of Congress Control Number: 2017905518
Published November 2017
v. 1.0

Printed in the United States of America
∞
This paper meets the requirements of
ANSI/NISO Z39.48-1992 (Permanence of Paper).

**BRU BAKER** got her first taste of life as a writer at the tender age of four, when she started publishing a weekly newspaper for her family. What they called nosiness she called a nose for news, and no one was surprised when she ended up with degrees in journalism and political science and started a career in journalism.

Bru spent more than a decade writing for newspapers before making the jump to fiction. She now works in reference and readers' advisory in a Midwestern library, though she still finds it hard to believe someone's willing to pay her to talk about books all day. Most evenings you can find her curled up with a book or her laptop. Whether it's creating her own characters or getting caught up in someone else's, there's no denying that Bru is happiest when she's engrossed in a story. She and her husband have two children, which means a lot of her books get written from the sidelines of various sports practices.

Website: www.bru-baker.com

Blog: www.bru-baker.blogspot.com

Twitter: @bru_baker

Facebook: www.facebook.com/bru.baker79

Goodreads: www.goodreads.com/author/show/6608093.Bru_Baker

Email: bru@bru-baker.com

## *By Bru Baker*

DREAMSPUN DESIRES
#31 – Tall, Dark, and Deported

DREAMSPUN BEYOND
#7 – Camp H.O.W.L.

Published by **DREAMSPINNER PRESS**
www.dreamspinnerpress.com

# Chapter One

**ADRIAN** was no stranger to putting on a good show. He was so good at swallowing his emotions and smiling that he doubted anyone realized how miserable he'd been for the last hour. From the moment he'd walked into the boardroom for a videoconference with the Portland office and seen the streamers hanging from the ceiling, he'd pasted a smile on his face and glad-handed every employee who'd come by to wish him well. Pretended his birthday was something worth celebrating rather than a reminder that eight years ago today should have been the happiest day of his life and instead had been the worst.

The promised videoconference hadn't been a lie. Only instead of seeing the quarterly budget projections he'd been expecting on the big screen, he'd been greeted by his family singing "Happy Birthday." The one saving grace was that the embarrassment had been limited to those family members who worked for the company—his cousins and aunts and uncles hadn't been dragged into the farce.

By the time the cake had been served and the conversation had dwindled, only Adrian and the Indianapolis marketing manager, Kurt, were left in the confetti-littered room. All in all it was a much more sedate party than his family would have thrown him back home, but it was still a painful reminder of a day he'd rather forget. Not that forgetting was possible. He lived with the consequences every day, and even though he'd made his peace with the way things were, he still struggled with feelings of isolation and loneliness, even when surrounded by his family.

His Pack—if a werewolf who wasn't actually a werewolf could have a Pack.

"Sorry about all this," Kurt said, gesturing at the mess around them. "You hadn't said anything about it being your birthday, so I figured you were going for low-key, but Sandra insisted, and you know how that goes."

Adrian snorted at the understatement. Kurt didn't know that the woman he was talking about was not only the CEO of Rothschild Architects but also the Pacific Northwest's Alpha werewolf. Her no-nonsense attitude and ruthless ambition were good for a lot more than pressuring their Indianapolis office into throwing her son a surprise birthday party. She was also the head of the West Coast Werewolf Tribunal and one of the scariest Alphas out there when it came to enforcing the code that kept their kind hidden and safe.

So yes, Adrian knew exactly how persistent the CEO could be when she wanted something. His mother was a force to be reckoned with, and he should have known ducking out of town over his birthday wouldn't grant him a reprieve from celebrations.

"I'm well aware."

"I lobbied to leave it at the cake," Kurt continued, seeming oblivious to Adrian's brittle mood. "But then the box of decorations showed up yesterday. I figured we'd better just go with it, no matter how over-the-top it seemed."

The streamers had definitely been over-the-top. Adrian scowled as dangling crepe paper whispered over his skin, the sensation sending an eerie shiver down his spine. He'd been on edge all day today, more so than he usually was on his birthday, and that was saying a lot. Maybe spending the day away from his Pack hadn't been a good idea after all.

Adrian took a breath and tried to let go of some of the tension hunching his shoulders. None of this was Kurt's fault, and he didn't deserve to be the scapegoat for Adrian's annoyance with his mother.

"Don't worry about it," he said, trying his hardest to soften his words. He poured his frustration into snatching the streamers from the ceiling, crumpling them in his fist. "I'll get the rest of it. You go on and head out for the night. I'll see you tomorrow."

Adrian had to admire his mother's ingenuity even as he was digging confetti out of the carpet pile. He'd saved himself the usual hullabaloo at home by scheduling this trip over his birthday, but instead of suffering through the usual to-do with the Pack, he'd substituted fresh humiliation in front of strangers. At least none of them were werewolves. It was easier to hide his exasperation and sadness from humans than it was from werewolf noses.

Not for the first time, he wondered if the way his family went overboard for his birthday was to compensate for their own guilt and sadness at his inability to shift. Not that it was their fault. A quirk of genetics is what the doctors his mother'd called in had said. All five of them.

Adrian ran a hand through his hair, recoiling in disgust when his fingers unearthed Silly String he'd missed on his last pass through. The head of human resources had been a little too enthusiastic in her celebrating, apparently. The fragile calm he'd managed to find shattered, and he pulled it from his hair with angry swipes, taking more than a few strands of hair with it.

He brushed the mess into the trash can, wrinkling his nose. Was that what he had to look forward to? Losing his hair? His knees already creaked when he got out of bed in the morning, an he'd swear he'd seen hair on his back when he looked in the mirror after his shower this morning. The men in his family had always tended toward hairiness, but that had skipped him. At the ripe old age of twenty-seven, he was the most baby-faced member of the Pack, even though he had two younger brothers.

The video screen on the wall flashed, catching his attention. He hesitated, wondering exactly how much shit he'd be in if he ignored it. A lot, probably. His family was already angry at him for leaving over his birthday; it was probably best not to poke the bear—or wolf, as it were—with something as petty as rejecting a call.

He leaned over to the center of the table and hit the Accept button. His sister Eliza's face filled the screen.

"Thanks a lot for the heads-up about the party," he said, saluting Kurt with the wastebasket he'd been collecting streamers and confetti in.

"That's not on me, kid," she said with a smirk. "Mom didn't tell anyone here until we'd already gathered for the meeting. Though in hindsight, it was odd she only invited members of the Pack to a quarterly budget meeting."

Rothschild Architects employed a good portion of the werewolves who lived in Portland, and they'd all been there for the party. Even so, Weres were only a small percentage of the firm's employees. With offices in three states, Rothschild had a lot more humans on the payroll than werewolves. His mother was a big proponent of hiding in plain sight.

"Bullshit," Adrian muttered. "Mom doesn't so much as sneeze these days without having you there to watch."

Eliza was his mother's second-in-command. Many Alphas ruled their Packs well into their golden years, but recently his mother had been preparing Eliza to take over as Alpha so she could focus more on her work with the Werewolf Tribunal.

"Whoa, take it down a notch," Eliza said. "Or else I'm not going to do my duty as a loving big sister and pass on a warning about what Mom has planned for tomorrow night."

He grimaced and rolled his shoulders to try to dispel some of the tension that had settled there. Eliza was right. He *was* overreacting. Adrian had been spoiling for a fight all day for absolutely no reason.

"Now, do you want to know what Mom has planned or not?"

"Doesn't matter. My flight's been delayed," he said.

Eliza rolled her eyes. "Don't tell me now. I have to be able to be surprised when you call breathlessly tomorrow with that excuse."

Adrian laughed, his first real smile all day cracking his face. "No, really. They already texted about it. I'm on a later flight tomorrow. I won't make it back until after midnight, so whatever Mom is planning is going to have to wait."

"I don't like the idea of you flying tomorrow at all," Eliza said, scrunching up her nose. "But a late flight? Are you sure about that?"

He hated flying. Everyone in the Pack did. While he might not be a werewolf physically, he'd been raised as one, and he'd inherited all their quirks. A hatred of crowded spaces was one of them.

"I can handle a full moon, Liz," Adrian said, scowling at the screen.

"I know you *can*, dipshit, but that doesn't mean you should."

In truth he'd forgotten there was a full moon tomorrow night. That explained some of his restlessness. Werewolves weren't slaves to the moon to the extent popular culture portrayed them to be, but it did have some pull over them. He might not sprout fur and claws, but he'd always been sensitive to it. Spending hours stuck in a tin can was not his idea of fun on the best of days, but Eliza was right—flying during a full moon would be a nightmare. All Adrian risked exposing was his bitchy side, but he still didn't relish the thought of being stuck on a plane with that going on.

"I'll be fine." The protest sounded weak even to him. Luckily, Eliza picked up on it.

"I don't like to pull rank, but I'm going to do it here. You're not flying tomorrow, Adrian. Change your flight and come home after the moon. Spending a day in a hotel room isn't ideal, but it's a hell of a lot better than being cooped up on a plane."

Relief shot through him. Biology might not compel him to follow her directions like it would a normal member of the Pack, but custom did. That and a sense of self-preservation—both because he didn't want to be on the plane and because he was afraid of what kind of revenge his sister would enact if he disobeyed. She wasn't as ruthless as their mother, but she was more creative.

"You're so bossy," he teased. "You'll explain to Mom?"

"God. Figures you'd stick me with the hard job." Eliza sniffed. "Consider it your birthday present."

Adrian laughed and shook his head, dislodging another piece of Silly String. "One, I'm doing this on a direct order from you, baby Alpha. And two, you never buy me a birthday present anyway."

Eliza growled, her eyes flashing at the teasing insult. As the oldest child of the Alpha, it was assumed she would inherit the title, but it hadn't been a given. Not until she'd demonstrated the necessary personality—bitchiness, bossiness, and a stubborn streak you could drive a car through—starting at around age three.

"It's Alpha-elect now," she said. "We had the ceremony last night."

Adrian swallowed hard. They'd conducted official Pack business without him? Jesus. And his mother said his problems were all in his head. Clearly not, if they were actually holding ceremonies in his absence now.

"Thanks for the invitation," he snapped, then instantly regretted it. It wouldn't have been her call. That was all on his mother.

Eliza's face fell. "I'm sorry. I wanted you there, but…."

She didn't have to fill in the blank for him. There was no reason for a human member of a werewolf Pack to be at a ceremony. He didn't share the biological bond with them the other adult werewolves did. He'd have been a spectator, nothing else.

"Sure," he said, looking away to gather himself. It stung more than it should, especially since he skipped Pack meetings by his own choice more often than not. What was the point, after all? He was human. "Congratulations."

"Thanks," she said quietly. "I'll talk to Mom about your flight. Stay safe. And happy birthday."

"Yeah, yeah," he said, waving off the unwanted sentiment with a sigh. "See you in a few days."

## Chapter Two

"**FOR** the last time, Ryan, we aren't keeping you prisoner here. You're an adult, and if you choose to leave, we can't stop you."

They really couldn't. The kids Tate worked with at Camp H.O.W.L. weren't prisoners—they were werewolves who were adjusting to their wolves. Technically, since the change came on the first full moon after a werewolf's nineteenth birthday, they weren't kids either. Everyone at the camp was a legal adult, but it was often difficult to tell from the way they acted.

Camp H.O.W.L. catered to the elite in werewolf society. A month at the camp cost more than a year's tuition at most colleges. He'd heard rumors that some parents signed their kids up as soon as they were born and started paying the exorbitant fee in monthly installments nearly two decades before their precious little wolflings would ever set foot on the manicured grounds.

It wasn't amenities like the raw juice bar or the Pilates machines that kept the kids from leaving camp, though. Every single one of them knew they'd be roasted by their Alpha if they walked away before the counselors released them. Guarding their secret from exposure was every werewolf's highest priority, even these stuck-up, pampered pseudoadults. And if any of them thought they knew best and tried to leave, well, that was between the werewolf and their Pack. In his seven years at the camp, Tate had never seen a werewolf leave before they graduated. There had been a few close calls, but all it had taken was a few words with the recalcitrant werewolf's Alpha to turn things around.

Tate had Ryan's Alpha on speed dial, since it was his job to know how to spot trouble. Tate hoped it wouldn't go that far, but it was a nice ace up his sleeve.

Ryan had his phone in his hand, his fingers clutched around the nearly indestructible case most of the kids arrived with. They weren't fashionable, but the wolf-proof titanium was a necessity while the young wolves learned how to deal with their heightened strength and volatile mood swings.

"I'm waiting on an Uber," Ryan sneered, his gaze locked on Tate's in blatant challenge.

Tate held up his hands to placate the teen. "That's your call, man," he said, trying his damnedest to project an air of calm detachment. Ryan's senses weren't honed enough yet to pick up on Tate's racing heart or the faint tang of salt in the air from the cold sweat trickling down his back.

He'd gotten an Uber? Jesus Christ. Someday these kids were going to be the death of him. An emotional, angry baby werewolf in an Uber?

Luckily they were miles and miles from the area's only Uber driver, and that was only if Wade Watkins could get his scuffed-up Ford F-150 to start in the wet autumn chill. A kid like Ryan would probably take one look at the dented, rusted-out truck and turn tail and run. Assuming Wade was even looking for a fare this time of night.

Ryan waved his phone at Tate, his lip trembling. "When my father finds out—"

Tate shook his head. "Your father knows exactly what happens at camp. In fact, he gets a detailed report about your progress every evening."

Today's report had included a carefully worded paragraph about Ryan's inability to control his shift, a problem compounded by his laziness and disrespectful attitude. Not that Tate had used those words.

Ryan has a strong sense of self but continues to struggle with impulsivity and has yet to find a way to apply his considerable will to controlling the finer aspects of his shift.

Translation: your son is a self-centered asshole who could give two shits about all the exercises we're teaching him because he can't be bothered to try to exert any self-control at all.

And since Ryan couldn't return to his family in New York until he'd stopped randomly sprouting fur and fangs at all hours of the day and night, he was going to have the dubious honor of a stay at Camp H.O.W.L. extended by an extra month—through September.

Ryan had gotten the news tonight. It hadn't gone well. The campers tended to form deep bonds with their cabin mates, and while Ryan's attitude had kept him from making any bosom buddies, his pride had taken a considerable hit when the rest of his cabin departed earlier that afternoon, leaving him by his lonesome until the next crop of kids came in for the full moon tomorrow. It sucked, and Tate couldn't blame the kid for being angry. Maybe he'd apply that toward actually learning what he'd been sent to camp to master this time around.

Tate fought back the ripple of his own frustration shivering down his spine, threatening to leave fur in its wake. "If you want to leave, we'll arrange to have someone from your Pack come pick you up."

Ryan scoffed. "I already told you, I have an Uber."

Tate sent up a silent prayer for patience. "And where would the Uber take you, Ryan? All the way back to New York? That's quite the trip."

Ryan's lip stopped trembling and arched into an impressive sneer. "The airport. My dad will send the jet."

Because of course this whelp's family would have a private jet.

Tate took a deep breath and tried to channel the camp's meditation instructor. Quinn was always going on about helping the kids find their inner Zen. No wonder they were all so testy all the time—what the hell was inner Zen? He'd rather find his inner Netflix. Something Ryan's late-night tantrum was keeping him from.

"Let's call your dad," Tate offered. "That way we can make sure he sends the plane and you aren't left waiting at the airport."

There was no way in hell Ryan's father would send a plane. He was the Alpha of New York City, and he wasn't going to bend to his nineteen-year-old son's whim. Tate had already had the pleasure of talking to the man this morning when he and the rest of the counselors had decided Ryan wasn't ready to be released. It hadn't been pleasant, but Tate was sure that even though Ryan's father wasn't Tate's biggest fan, he'd back him up on this count. No one wanted a teenage werewolf with poor control on the loose in a major city.

"My dad doesn't have time for something this trivial," Ryan said, but his voice wavered.

Tate took a good look at him, and where a stubborn, condescending man had stood a moment before, Tate could only see a scared little boy. Forget the fact that this "boy" was nineteen and well over six feet tall. Everything about his posture screamed he was on the defensive, and his voice had cracked when he'd mentioned his dad.

Tate was pretty far removed from Alpha politics, by deliberate choice and by virtue of both his position at the camp and how isolated they were. Being on staff at Camp H.O.W.L. gave him an excuse to keep himself out of werewolf drama. The camp was a neutral space where kids from feuding Packs could come without fear of repercussions—it had to be a safe place. And if the by-product of that made the camp safe for a Packless werewolf like Tate, well, so much the better. Very few people knew he wasn't part of a Pack. He'd disclosed it to the former camp director when he'd applied almost a decade ago, but he didn't think the man had said anything to his successor when she took over a few years back. The camp doctor knew, since being unaffiliated had a few potential medical and psychological repercussions. But as far as Tate knew, no one else—aside from his former Pack, of course—knew he was on his own.

It was a rare thing, coming upon a werewolf who had no Pack affiliation. And to be honest, it wasn't something he'd wish for anyone who wasn't in his very specific situation. The only reason it worked for him was his position here at the camp. His coworkers and even the kids formed an unofficial Pack of sorts, and it was enough of a bond to get him through those difficult moons.

Tate took another look at Ryan, paying closer attention than usual to his posture and expression. Ryan had come to camp over a month ago as a sneering, privileged brat, and he'd worked hard to sustain that image over the following weeks. Everything Ryan had done in his time at Camp H.O.W.L. had screamed Alpha male, and Tate had allowed his dislike for the way Ryan acted to color his perceptions. Right now, he didn't look like a self-assured, arrogant would-be Alpha. Tate would bet if he researched Ryan's Pack, he'd find several older siblings who were in line for their father's title ahead of Ryan. Maybe even cousins as well. There was nothing Alpha-like about his bowed shoulders and the scared glint in his eyes now.

Had he been approaching Ryan wrong all along? Tate took a careful step closer, relieved when Ryan didn't bolt.

"I doubt your father would think a call from you would be a bother," he said, taking care to make his tone even and nonthreatening. "I talked to him earlier today, and it's obvious he loves you very much."

Ryan flinched at the mention of Tate's morning phone call. Had his father called him afterward? He'd seemed accepting of the situation when Tate had talked to him, but that could have been Alpha posturing—like the kind he'd thought Ryan had been engaging in all month.

"He has a huge Pack to run and a business he's in charge of. He doesn't have time to deal with something like this," Ryan muttered. He kept his gaze locked on the toe of his shoe, which he was dragging through the gravel at the mouth of the trail that led to the parking lot. It's where Tate had found him after staff realized he was missing and sent up the alarm.

Tate didn't think the kid had actually intended to leave. If he had, surely he'd have made it farther than this. He had a considerable head start, and even if he was hell-bent on calling an Uber, he could have done it from the road. With the benefit of werewolf speed, Ryan could have easily gotten several miles away before anyone noticed. Instead, he'd only made it the quarter of a mile to the lot.

"Your safety and wellbeing aren't things your father needs to 'deal with,'" Tate said softly. "You aren't an inconvenience to him. He's concerned because you're taking a bit longer than the average werewolf to gain control, but that's a minor thing, Ryan. No one is judging you."

Well, that wasn't strictly true. Tate and the rest of the staff were judging him—but it was because of his attitude and his refusal to comply with the training and take the classes seriously. They'd never harshly judge a camper who was really trying. Kids like Ryan who were more focused on disruptions and disrespecting the counselors than putting in the work were the exception, but even those kids were generally driven by something unseen—like a fear of their Alpha, body image issues that had plagued them before the Turn but worsened after, or a severe lack of self-confidence that kept them from succeeding because of crippling doubt. Only a very few were simply bad eggs, and up until tonight Tate had Ryan pegged as one of those.

Maybe he'd made a mistake there. He might have more in common with Ryan than he'd realized. Ryan showed all the signs of having an overbearing, controlling Alpha, though Tate hoped that's where the similarities ended. God help any wolfling who'd had a childhood as abusive as his own.

"My brothers were fine," Ryan said, bitterness seeping into his voice. "They were here, like, a week before everything settled. My sister could control her shift by the end of the night she Turned. I'm the family embarrassment in everything else, but I figured this would be one area where I could actually keep up. Guess not."

Tate wished they weren't having this conversation in the parking lot, but beggars couldn't be choosers. He'd been trying to get Ryan to open up for weeks, and he wasn't about to tell the kid he had to come by during office hours tomorrow to continue. The minute Ryan walked away from him, he'd lose the entire thread and no progress would be made.

"Why would you say you're an embarrassment? You seem like a bright guy, and you're very popular here at camp."

Ryan scoffed. "No one here really knows anything about me. I don't have any friends in the Pack at home because they all know what a screwup I am."

Tate made a mental note to call someone in Ryan's Pack other than his father to find out more about his Pack life. He wasn't terribly surprised to hear Ryan had problems—being the Alpha's child set a wolfling apart, and growing up with as much money and privilege as Ryan had would have a similar effect. He'd been insulated from humans his entire life, and it sounded like his Pack had kept him at a distance as well. No wonder the kid was so poorly adjusted.

Tate chose his words carefully. He hadn't been blowing smoke when he said Ryan was a smart kid. He'd jump all over it if Tate tried to pander to him, so he took the chance with blunt honesty instead.

"Sometimes people who have a good deal of power or money have a hard time making friends," he offered. "People want to be near them for the status, not for true friendship. That can be very isolating. And growing up like that can bring about self-esteem problems that interfere with conquering the change."

Ryan was silent, but he wasn't protesting or disagreeing.

"Do you think that might be what's happening here?"

Tate wasn't prepared for Ryan to snarl and lunge toward the trees, his clothes shredding as fur sprouted and muscle and sinew twisted and reformed. He watched Ryan go, relieved he at least had the sense to head back toward camp instead of into the parking lot.

They kept a large perimeter around Camp H.O.W.L. Ryan's Uber wouldn't have been able to pick him up in the parking lot without a staff member jogging two miles down the pebbled lane to open the high-tech gate they kept locked twenty-four seven.

Ryan would be safe enough, but Tate would still stop by the lodge to tell the unlucky soul who'd drawn security duty for the night there was an angry wolfling prowling around. The entire forest was blanketed with night-vision cameras and motion sensors, and an alarm would sound in the security room if Ryan made it close to the electric fence that lined the perimeter of the camp. That's what had alerted them to his presence in the parking lot in the first place.

Tate wished they'd had more time to talk before Ryan shifted, but they'd still accomplished a lot tonight. Ryan hadn't successfully completed a full Turn since his birthday over a month ago, so his transformation tonight was a milestone. Now they'd have to work on getting him there without needing to invoke such strong emotions. The Turn would come easier these next few days because of the full moon, which was tomorrow night, but Tate was sure that now Ryan had the confidence boost of being able to successfully Turn, he'd be able to do it again. Then they'd work on forcing the change—and holding it back—at will.

But that was for another day. Tate was going to get himself a congratulatory beer after checking in with the security detail and settle in for some quality time with his Netflix. He hated seeing any wolfling in distress, but the ones who shivered and shrank when they mentioned their Alpha were the worst.

*That's not me*, he told himself firmly. And it wasn't. Not anymore at least.

Tate couldn't change the fact he'd been terrorized by his Alpha growing up, but he had the power to change his present and his future. And he had. He'd renounced his ties to the Pack almost fifteen years ago.

A run would probably settle Tate's nerves better than anything, but he didn't want to chance crossing paths with Ryan. The wolfling had shifted involuntarily and bolted to get away from him—Tate wasn't going to cut whatever solace the exertion might be giving Ryan by popping up on the trail.

Tate rolled his shoulders and stretched, trying to ease the tension gathered there. Maybe he'd let himself into the camp gym instead of heading to his cabin to watch Netflix. There wasn't much that working up a good old-fashioned sweat couldn't cure.

## *Chapter Three*

**ADRIAN** laced his running shoes, glad he'd second-guessed himself and tossed them in his bag at the last minute. He worked long hours when he traveled, making the most of his time at the satellite offices so he could minimize the number of trips he had to take each year. He always booked hotels with fitness centers with the hope he'd be able to get a long run on the treadmill in after finishing up in the evening.

He hardly ever did. Usually he was so exhausted from the long day and the constant socializing that he holed up in his room and mainlined Candy Crush until he fell asleep.

But today was different. He'd been at the office all day, including the humiliating surprise birthday party and the dinner the management staff had insisted on treating him to afterward. The only saving grace there was he didn't think the dinner invitation had been part of his mother's party directive, which made it easier to bear. Surprisingly, he'd found himself having fun getting to know some of the staff on a personal level, finding out things about people he'd worked with from a distance for years.

The urban planning director was an avid runner, and she'd been the one to suggest he take time out to run along the canal and the cultural trail to see some of the sights in Indianapolis after he'd shared that he ran several half marathons a year. His last had been the Rock 'n' Roll Seattle half marathon in June, and things had gotten so busy he hadn't had a good long run since. Given that it was the end of August now, that was a long time to go for him.

Kristen had given him directions to the start of the cultural trail, which she'd said was about eight miles long and included a scenic portion along the city's canal. He hadn't even known Indianapolis *had* a canal, but apparently it was pretty close to the hotel he was staying in.

Adrian double-knotted his shoes and stood to stretch. He worked at a standing desk back in Portland, but the Indianapolis office didn't have any, so he'd spent the day hunched over a desk. His shoulders were stiff, and the light stretch felt good. Running would feel even better, he thought.

He'd been keyed up all day, and instead of his energy waning like it usually did at the end of a long workday, he was more pumped up than ever. Adrian wasn't sure where all this nervous energy was coming from, but he was going to take advantage of it and indulge in a longer-than-usual run tonight. It had been weeks since he'd done more than a quick three or four miles, so he intended to explore every inch of this eight-mile trail.

He pocketed his hotel key card and tucked his phone into a pouch in his running shorts. He usually liked to listen to music when he ran, but he was actually looking forward to soaking up some silence tonight.

Well, as much silence as being in the heart of a city could afford him. Plus he didn't like having headphones in to distract him when he was running in an unfamiliar place, especially at night. Kristen had assured him the trail was well lit, and the sun was still up. He doubted it would be by the time he finished, but he had a good half hour of daylight left.

He pulled the door closed behind him, wincing as it slammed. He hadn't meant to put that much force behind it.

He was on the thirty-second floor of his hotel, a monstrous iridescent blue building out of place among the other buildings in the Indianapolis skyline. It looked modern and sleek, which could be great somewhere else. But across the street from the brick baseball field where the Indians played and next to the stately limestone buildings and museums around it, it stuck out like a sore thumb and made the urban planner in him wince.

Adrian hopped in place while he waited for the elevator, his muscles practically screaming to be let loose on a run. He couldn't remember a time he'd anticipated dashing off quite this much, and that was odd. He had to start making exercise a priority if this was how his body responded to being deprived of it.

The elevator dinged, and he indulged in one last hop and stretch before entering the empty car, glad there wasn't anyone to make small talk with. That would likely change on his ride down, but he'd take the calm silence for now.

**ADRIAN** never slept well in hotels, but last night's restlessness took his insomnia to a new level. He'd come back from his run with the pleasant buzz he usually felt after exerting himself on a short run, not the exhaustion and satisfying soreness he usually felt after a longer one. Having gone weeks without running a long distance, he should have been achy and cramping when he finished the eight-mile trail, but he'd come back barely out of breath and, if anything, more keyed up than he'd been when he started.

To make matters worse, the hotel had been ridiculously loud all night, with people clomping up and down the hallways at all hours and talking stridently in other rooms. The elevator was so noisy he was almost afraid to take it in the morning for fear it was about to break down.

The hotel had been perfectly quiet and calm before last night, when things seemed to explode. Sometimes literally. He could have sworn he'd heard something shatter in the next room around 3:00 a.m.

It had been impossible for him to relax enough to sleep, and even when he'd passed out due to sheer exhaustion in the wee hours of the morning, it hadn't been for long. He'd caught snatches of sleep through the night, which might have been worse for him than staying up the entire time. At least he felt like it had been worse. Who knew how bad he'd be feeling if he hadn't managed even the meager amount of sleep he'd gotten?

Hell, this was worse than the time he'd had to spend a weekend sharing a hotel with an entire league of youth hockey teams.

Even the restaurant was louder than it had been the first few days of his stay. Adrian's head throbbed with lack of sleep and undercaffeination since he hadn't been able to stomach either the noise or the smells in the hotel's restaurant this morning. He'd forgone the breakfast buffet he'd enjoyed the last two days and opted to grab a coffee on his walk to the office instead.

"Venti Caramel Macchiato, extra shot, no whip for Aaron?"

Adrian blinked blearily, struggling to focus past the tightening band of his tension headache. The girl at the counter looked at him expectantly.

"Venti for Aaron?" she said again, waving the drink. "Extra shot, no whip."

It was the right drink but the wrong name, and when no one else stepped up he surged forward clumsily.

"A little advice, Aaron? You drink too many of these and you're gonna have a heart attack," she said when he reached out for it. "That's four shots. Nobody needs four shots."

Maybe Aaron didn't need four shots, but Adrian most definitely did. He grunted out a noncommittal agreement and took it from her. He felt halfway to a heart attack anyway, so surely the coffee could only help.

He'd been feverish when he woke up, and since then he'd swung back and forth between cold sweats and pins and needles all over his body. If he didn't know better, he'd say he had a hangover between his pounding head and the way his stomach had roiled at the scent of breakfast. But he'd called it an early night after his run and relaxed in bed with a minibar snack that had definitely *not* included any sort of alcohol.

Adrian took a sip of his coffee as he stopped at a crosswalk and waited for the light to change. He nearly heaved when the bitter liquid spilled across his tongue. He'd ordered this drink dozens of times, and it had always been sweet and smooth. Nothing like this awful concoction. The taste of burned coffee lingered in his mouth, held there by a syrupy residue he could feel like a weight against his tongue.

He scraped his tongue against his teeth, trying to rid himself of the sensation. This entire day had been a nightmare, and he'd only been up for an hour. Even the hot shower he'd taken to try to loosen his tense muscles and ease his headache had been a disaster. The hotel must have been having water pressure problems because the rain showerhead had been anything but relaxing. The water had hit his skin like tiny missiles, leaving him feeling tender and raw afterward.

The light changed, and Adrian moved across the wide street with the smattering of people who'd been waiting near him. The man closest to him must have had his Bluetooth headset turned up to eleven—Adrian could hear every word. He glanced over, surprised the nicely dressed businessman wasn't more concerned about privacy. From what Adrian had heard, it sounded like the man was listening to an audiobook or podcast describing a sex scene in lurid detail. No one around them looked the slightest bit scandalized, which made Adrian reevaluate some of his assumptions about Indianapolis. The book would have raised some eyebrows even in his liberal hometown of Portland, but it got nary a sideways glance here in the Heartland. Adrian hadn't felt this embarrassed about sex since

the Werewolf Tribunal-mandated sex-ed class he'd
had to take when he turned eighteen. All wolflings
were required to take the class before the Turn, and it
had been hell on earth squirming in discomfort as an
eighty-year-old female werewolf droned on about the
nuances of werewolf sex.

Lost in thought, Adrian brought his foot down
hard on the curb and almost went sprawling. The
businessman he'd been watching grabbed him by the
elbow and kept him on his feet, but Adrian's satchel
swung forward and slammed into the man and the
impact knocked one of his earbuds out.

Adrian's face flamed when a long, loud moan
split the air, but no one noticed. The businessman gave
him a concerned glance once he'd steadied Adrian on
the sidewalk, but Adrian waved him off with a quick
thanks. The book continued to play, muted slightly
when the man tucked the earbud back into place.

The world seemed to slow, his vision reduced to
sparkling dust motes and the swirl of exhaust from a
passing bus. Adrian stumbled to a stop, slack-jawed.
No one had heard. That's why they hadn't reacted.
Because the man had been listening at normal volume,
and even when the earbud had fallen out, no one had
noticed because it hadn't been audible.

Except *he'd* heard.

Adrian rubbed his hand across his face and stepped
to the side to avoid the tide of people. What was going
on? He was used to seeing his Packmates react to
things outside the register he could process, but he'd
obviously never experienced it himself.

Had that been the problem at the hotel too? Maybe
a herd of elephants *hadn't* moved into the room above

his. Maybe he'd just been hearing normal footsteps, amplified to an almost unbearable level for him.

He'd never given much thought to what werewolf senses must be like. Sure, he'd seen his sister flinch when fire alarms went off, or noticed how irritable his family could get when they were in a loud, crowded restaurant. But mostly, the werewolves he knew adapted to their heightened senses. Most werewolves always carried earplugs with them and invested in fancy noise-canceling headphones to help them focus when they needed to. The walls in the house he grew up in had been soundproofed, as was standard in most werewolf households. And they avoided apartment buildings and condos like the plague.

If he'd been experiencing enhanced werewolf hearing last night, he couldn't blame the people on the next floor. His upstairs neighbors in his apartment at home sometimes drove him nuts with their high heels and vacuuming, but that was nothing like what he'd been tortured with last night.

That couldn't be what was happening, though. He didn't know of anyone who had werewolf senses but lacked the ability to shift. Not that he personally knew anyone born to werewolf parents who was a human—like him.

Young wolflings were essentially human—the hormones that prompted the shift weren't produced until they went through their second puberty on the first full moon after their nineteenth birthday. Before that, they were vulnerable to human illnesses and needed human vaccinations. Blood tests revealed nothing spectacular about them. But after their second puberty, the Turn as they called it, the hormones that drove the shift were detectable in their blood.

When he'd failed to Turn, Adrian had seen a parade of doctors. He'd had scores of tests and second and even third opinions. His mother had refused to accept the diagnosis until she'd hauled him to a werewolf endocrinologist. The results had been conclusive, and his family had been horrified. There was no room for doubt. Adrian's blood had no traces of anything outside the norm. He was perfectly healthy—and 100 percent human.

Adrian flexed his fingers and stared at the back of his hand. He wasn't experiencing any kind of surge in strength—just the enhancement of his senses. Which could be explained by something much more mundane, like illness.

He swallowed hard, fighting nausea from the scent of the cooling coffee he was still holding. His head continued to pound, and his muscles and joints ached. Surely he was coming down with the flu. That had to be it. Maybe he'd hallucinated the audiobook and the smell of the coffee. God knew he'd listened to his siblings complain about their super senses enough to be able to imagine it.

Adrian was due to leave tomorrow, and he'd planned to spend today tweaking things at the office and meeting with staffers. But he wouldn't be doing anyone any favors if he got them all sick. Maybe the better choice would be to retreat back to the hotel. He'd already extended his reservation through the full moon, but he could push it out a few more days. He certainly didn't want to fly while he was feeling like this, whatever *this* was. A bus passed, and Adrian's stomach roiled at the scent of the fumes. Decision made, he did an about-face and turned back to the stoplight. He'd head back to the hotel and take a nap.

Maybe that would help. Adrian clenched his hands, recoiling when he felt the bite of sharp fingernails into his skin. The ferrous scent of blood made him gag. He shouldn't be strong enough to break the skin so easily. And he definitely shouldn't be able to smell such a small amount of blood. He couldn't explain this away as the flu. He was definitely Turning.

A wave of dizziness sent his head spinning as he crossed the street, but this time there wasn't a kindly businessman nearby to stop his fall. Adrian went down hard, right in the middle of the crosswalk.

*Shit*, he thought right before his head hit the pavement.

# *Chapter Four*

**"YOU'RE** sure?"

Tate tapped his foot impatiently, craning his neck over the desk in an attempt to see what the camp director was writing. He couldn't read the woman's scrawl under the best of circumstances, so he didn't know why he'd even tried to decipher it upside down.

He'd been annoyed when a breathless camper had barged into his session with another wolfling to deliver a summons to Anne Marie's office. Tate might feel like he spent a lot of his time herding cattle, like a normal camp counselor would, but in reality, the bulk of his time was spent helping wolflings work through psychological issues that either impacted their shift or just weighed heavily on their minds. Most of these kids had never been away from home, and that led to a lot of homesickness and anxiety on top of the usual issues werewolf puberty brought on: an uptick in aggression, irritability, and the mental horror of dealing with an influx of new sensory inputs.

Tate had assumed when the camper had burst in there must be an emergency. There was literally no other reason anyone would interrupt a counselor who was in session with a wolfling. He'd made his apologies to the camper and rushed over to the administration building, only to find himself shushed and made to wait by Anne Marie, who was in the middle of a phone call.

Tate looked up when another counselor rushed in, looking as frazzled as he was sure he had a few minutes ago when he'd been the one to skid to a halt in Anne Marie's office.

"Evan said it was a code forty-five," Harris said, his breath coming hard from his apparent run to the building. His offices were the farthest from the administration building. Tate had only had to dash across the quad, but Harris would have had to cover almost half a mile. Given that only seven minutes had passed since a camper had knocked on Tate's door, Harris's hustle was impressive.

"A breach?" Tate's eyebrows shot up. Had Ryan managed to find a way into town after all? He'd met with the kid this morning, and things had seemed okay. Not great, but he couldn't expect miracles. The wolfling had at least seemed calmer and more focused on his classes.

Harris shrugged and eyed Anne Marie warily. "That's what Evan said. He didn't know what it meant, thank God, but he'd overheard Anne Marie saying those words on the phone when she'd asked him to grab me."

Evan must have shifted to run with the message. Tate made a mental note to congratulate the kid on his control later. It would have been difficult to center himself enough to shift amid that kind of anxiety.

Anne Marie hung up the phone before Tate could grill Harris for more information. They both turned to her, bodies tensed as they awaited instructions. There was a reason they had yearly training drills and protocols for situations like this one In the case of a shifted wolf on the loose in town, Harris was the go-to guy since he had trained as a volunteer forest ranger and had a good relationship with the forestry service in the area. If it was an unshifted teen out talking about wolves, any of the counselors had credentials they could flash at local authorities to take custody of the kids. On paper, Camp H.O.W.L. was a private juvenile detention and rehabilitation center for troubled teens.

Which was actually true, after a fashion. They were just troubled by a furry change instead of legal or emotional problems. Even the camp name had a human cover story. The acronym stood for Honor, Obligation, Willpower, and Loyalty. All traits that would serve a miscreant human teenager and a werewolf equally well.

"I need you two to drive up to Indianapolis to pick up a camper," Anne Marie said, her irritation clear.

Tate opened his mouth to protest, but she cut him off with a wave of her hand.

"We have a werewolf who started the Turn last night but didn't realize it," she said. "He's at Methodist Hospital in Indy, admitted for fever and delusions. He passed out in the middle of the street and was taken in by ambulance. Luckily he had his Alpha as his emergency contact in his phone, and she realized what was happening. She called me."

Tonight was the full moon, which meant the kid would complete his Turn a few minutes after moonrise. That absolutely could not happen in a hospital. Tate did some quick mental calculations. If they left now, they should make it back with time to spare, assuming the hospital would release the kid to him.

"Why can't his Alpha pick him up? Surely they have a safe room," Harris said, his eyes narrowed.

"I'm sure they do," Anne Marie snapped. "But since his Pack is in Portland, that won't do anyone much good."

Portland? What the hell kind of Alpha would let a wolfling travel across the country right before his Turn? There were rules against things like that. The Tribunal could bring the Alpha up on charges.

Another piece of what Anne Marie had said fell into place, and Tate's mouth dropped open. From the grim line of Anne Marie's mouth, he could see she knew the significance as well. The head of the Tribunal was the Alpha of Portland. She was an outspoken advocate of protecting werewolf secrecy, and since she'd started her term, punishments for even minor infractions in the area had skyrocketed. This would be incredibly bad for her if it got out.

"It's her son," Anne Marie said, her voice dropping. "So I'm sure I don't have to tell you how important it is we handle this with discretion and tact."

"How could she—"

Tate cut Harris's outraged words off. "The Alpha of Portland only has three sons, and they're all well over nineteen."

This wasn't adding up. As a wolf without a Pack, he made it is his business to know the details about the governing Alphas and their policies. It could be dangerous for him to run afoul of an Alpha who had a vendetta against unaffiliated werewolves, so he made sure to know who those Alphas were.

Anne Marie nodded grimly. "Adrian Rothschild turned twenty-seven yesterday. Before last night, he had never exhibited any signs of the Turn. His Pack had accepted the fact that he was human—until now."

Tate's mind raced. Adrian was far from the first wolfborn who didn't Turn. They were considered a genetic mutation, and it was rare enough that many werewolves might not ever meet someone afflicted with it. But he hadn't known it was possible for them to Turn later in life.

"Wait, so there's a twenty-seven-year-old guy out there who didn't realize what was happening? Really?" Harris's tone was harsh.

Anne Marie looked like she agreed, but she didn't say anything.

It *was* hard to believe, but it had to be a complete mindfuck for the poor guy. Yes, senses came online first and signaled the start of the Turn, but if you'd spent almost ten years convinced you were human, would you jump to the conclusion you were Turning? Probably not. The mind was a complicated thing. It could—and often did—warp people's perceptions of feelings and events to make them fit reality as they knew it. The man likely thought he was getting sick. From what he'd heard, the early symptoms of the Turn were a lot like a human migraine. Maybe that's what Adrian had figured was happening to him. There would have been no reason for him to think he was Turning. It would be like a man with stomach pains assuming he was in labor—it didn't even register as a possibility.

"But he knows what's going on now, right?" Tate asked, finding his voice. "He's not going to fight us when we show up to take him?"

"No, he's awake and aware," Anne Marie said. "He's listed as delusional because he's reacting to noises that aren't there—or rather, that are there, I imagine, but are outside normal human hearing."

That was good. Tate had worried when Anne Marie said he was hospitalized with delusions that Adrian had talked about the werewolf community or told the doctors he thought he was a werewolf. Thank God for small favors.

Harris seemed to have worked past his disbelief and was now grabbing things they'd need for the drive from the supply closet outside Anne Marie's office—bottles of water, phone chargers, heavy-duty restraints, and a syringe with enough tranquilizer to down an elephant.

Tate sent up a quick, silent prayer to the universe that they would be able to get Adrian back to the camp before moonrise. He didn't want to tranq him.

Harris poked his head into the room, his arms full. "Are we going in officially, or will he be able to check himself out?"

If the hospital put Adrian on a twenty-four-hour psych hold, it could be difficult to get him discharged, but since both Tate and Harris were board-certified clinical psychologists, they might be able to get the hospital to release him to their care. It would have to be arranged as an official transfer to Camp H.O.W.L., and while they'd done that before in a few other cases, the camp was officially registered as a juvenile center, which would raise some eyebrows if anyone looked too closely at the paperwork. At twenty-seven, Adrian definitely wasn't a kid.

And that was a big part of the problem. There was no way to know how the Turn would affect him. This was new territory. Would he actually Turn and shift fully? Or would the heightened senses that had already manifested be the extent of his Turn? It was anyone's guess, since to Tate's knowledge, this kind of delayed Turn had never happened before.

"I don't know how messy the paperwork will be," Anne Marie admitted. "His family has already called the hospital and listed Tate as his psychologist of record, so we can only hope the facility will release him to you without problem."

"He's an adult, so there shouldn't be a problem unless his behavior is registering as disturbed enough to merit a hold," Tate said. He slung the bag full of water and snacks Harris handed him over his shoulder. Harris's own bag was full of the restraints, gags, and other things Tate hoped they wouldn't need. The soft restraints wouldn't cause Adrian any pain, but Tate hated using them on anyone. They brought up too many unpleasant memories.

"Since he's an adult, what are we going to do with him when we get him here?" Harris asked, his face clouded.

It wasn't undue concern, Tate decided. Adrian would likely be bigger and stronger than their campers, which would make them unmatchable as far as any physical training together was concerned. And besides, having a twenty-seven-year-old man bunk down with a bunch of teenagers wasn't appropriate.

"We'll deal with that when you get back," Anne Marie said. "The important thing right now is getting to him before the moon rises and he outs us all by Turning in the middle of a hospital."

That would be a disaster. Public Turns had happened before, and Tate was sure they would happen again, but that didn't make them an inconsequential thing. It took a lot of work to cover up something like that, and he had a feeling it would be a nearly impossible task if the location of the Turn was one of the busiest hospitals in a large city.

"His Alpha will want to talk to you. I'll have her call you while you're en route," Anne Marie added, which only made Tate's shoulders heavier. He hated dealing with Alphas on a good day, and this was definitely not a good day.

"We'll call you when we have him and we're headed back south," Harris said. He grabbed the strap of Tate's bag and tugged him along, pulling him out of Anne Marie's office.

"You make it sound like a kidnapping," Tate complained. He was already feeling uneasy for what they were about to do to this poor guy, and talking about it like they were going to blindfold him and toss him in a trunk wasn't helping.

Not that what they *were* going to do to him was much better. He'd likely have to be put in the soft restraints once they were on the road, and he might even need earplugs and a blindfold depending on how sensitive his hearing and vision had become. God help them if they got pulled over on the drive back to southern Indiana.

Harris grunted as he plucked a set of keys to one of the camp's vans from the hanger near the reception desk. "More like adultnapping," he said, sidestepping the kick Tate whipped out in response.

"I just hope he's happy to see us," Tate mumbled as they crunched down the same gravel path he'd followed Ryan on yesterday. "If he's so far gone we can't reason with him about why coming with us is the best option then things are really going to suck."

## Chapter Five

**ADRIAN** had given up on breathing through his nose hours ago. The scent of hospital antiseptic burned his nostrils and throat, but taking slow, measured breaths through his mouth seemed to mitigate it a bit. It also gave him something to focus on that wasn't the itching, crawling feeling of *wrongness* on his skin or the way his muscles contracted and spasmed of their own accord like they were preparing for something big.

They were, of course. He realized that now. It had dawned on him before he'd passed out like an idiot on the street this morning, but when he'd awakened in the ambulance, he'd been disoriented and confused again. He'd managed to tell the paramedics about his fever and headache, which he attributed his heightened senses to. It was probably a good thing he'd forgotten his prepavement revelation in those first few moments of consciousness—no doubt he'd have blurted everything out if he had.

He'd been almost himself again by the time the ambulance had screamed its way to the emergency room, but he could hardly have hopped out and excused himself. What could he have said? "I know these symptoms seem a lot like a stroke or an aneurysm, but actually it's just werewolf puberty setting in almost ten years late! LOL! I'll be on my way to go pop a fang in private, guys. Thanks for the ride."

Yeah, *that* would have gone over like gangbusters.

So he'd let himself be wheeled into the hospital. He hadn't had to fake his groans as the bright fluorescent lights tried to gouge out his eyeballs, or his twitches and spasms as his muscles clenched and released of their own accord. They'd recorded that as a seizure brought on by his high temperature, though Adrian knew the episodes were his body readying itself for the stretch of the Turn. Even his elevated temperature was part of the process. Something about the influx of hormones that caused the Turn fighting with his white blood cells.

He'd been able to hold them off from taking blood by claiming it was against his religion, as he and his siblings had been trained to do when they were young teens in their werewolf classes.

It had helped immensely that his mother had backed up his claim when the hospital had called her. As his emergency contact, she'd been called while he'd been en route in the ambulance, thanks to a nice paramedic who'd found his phone on him. His mother had laid the groundwork for his refusal of meds and tests, so when he'd reached the hospital, his paperwork had already noted his religious exemption in big block letters at the top.

Adrian knew his luck could only hold for so long. If the hospital found a reason to admit him against his will—the psych hold he'd heard doctors talking about down at the nurses' station, where they'd assumed he couldn't hear them—then all of that prep work would go out the window. They'd be able to override his wishes and draw blood and do whatever else they wanted.

He'd tried his damnedest to act normal after that. They needed him to be delusional or dangerous for a psych hold, so he'd been as docile as he could manage instead. It was getting harder as his headache worsened with every code called over the PA and every squeaky-wheeled gurney that rolled down the hall, but he was hanging in.

Adrian had talked to his mom about an hour ago, though they couldn't say much since there was always a nurse in the room with him. It was too dangerous to talk in code, so he'd simply told her he thought he'd gotten the flu. It was a much worse case than the one he'd gotten when he was nineteen, he'd told her. She'd caught on right away and assured him she knew people in the area who could help with flu remedies.

He'd felt a curious combination of relief and apprehension when she'd checked in an hour later and told him help was on the way. What kind of help? Were they werewolves she knew from the area? Tribunal officers? And what would they do with him? He'd heard enough Turning stories to know the environment a werewolf had his Turn in had a huge impact on how stressful the Turn was.

"Dr. Lewis is here to see you," the nurse who'd been camping out by his door informed him.

Adrian looked up, unsure of who that was. Was he getting the psych consult the nurse kept threatening him with? Was this the beginning of the end for him? What would the Tribunal do if he let his blood get taken? There was no way it would look normal this far into the Turn.

"Adrian, nice to see you," the doctor said as he walked in. He picked up the clipboard at the end of Adrian's bed and started flipping through it, eyes trained on it as he continued to speak. "Your mother tells me you have a particularly bad case of the flu. I'm sorry to hear that."

Adrian had tensed when the man walked in, but at those words he sank back into his nest of pillows and breathed a sigh of relief. Somehow his mother had found someone to impersonate a doctor to spring him from the hospital. He was impressed by her ingenuity, though she could have done a better job. The guy standing in the doorway looked nothing like a doctor. He was young, for starters, probably only a little older than Adrian himself. And he was wearing a tight T-shirt and jeans with a scruffy pair of Converses. Would it have been that difficult to find a white lab coat or a pair of scrubs?

But the nurse seemed to be swallowing it hook, line, and sinker, and that was the important part. She rushed to the man's side with another chart.

"His vitals have stabilized since he arrived, but he's refusing a blood draw or MRI. Temp has come down considerably, as has his blood pressure and pulse." She gave Adrian a quick, assessing look. "His pupil response is abnormal, but we haven't been able to rule out drugs since we can't get a draw."

Adrian started to protest but stopped before the words made it past his lips. Actually, it would be better if they thought he was a druggie. It was a convenient excuse for most of his symptoms.

"He was found in the street?" the not-doctor asked, his gaze coming up to examine Adrian.

The man was flat-out gorgeous, and Adrian couldn't help but bring a hand up to try to smooth his own hair in response to the scrutiny. He was sure he looked terrible.

"Head laceration that didn't require stitches," the nurse said. "He lost consciousness. Bystanders called the ambulance. He was out for an estimated ten minutes. Paramedics reported he was disoriented and a little aggressive upon regaining consciousness in the ambulance, but by the time he arrived here, he was no longer showing signs of being disoriented or altered."

*Altered*, Adrian thought. If only this nurse knew exactly how altered he was at the moment—not to mention how much more altered he'd be as soon as the moon rose.

The man holding the chart hummed thoughtfully and looked back at the pages in his hands, flipping through them again.

"His family has arranged for transport to another facility," he said in a professionally detached voice as he tucked the chart under one arm and signed the paperwork the nurse had handed him when he'd come in.

"You'll have to clear that with the hospitalist on duty," she said. "Dr. Ramirez will—"

"I've already talked with Dr. Ramirez. She signed off on Adrian's release. We have a transport vehicle in the ambulance bay," the man said.

The nurse balked. "Mr. Rothschild needs a psych workup. Dr. Ramirez wouldn't sign off on a release without one."

The man smiled blandly and held up a badge at the end of a lanyard Adrian hadn't noticed on his initial assessment. "As you can see, I'll be taking him to a facility that is more than equipped to administer a full psychological workup. I assure you Mr. Rothschild will not leave until we are sure he is no danger to himself or others." He paused and looked up to shoot a covert wink at Adrian. "And our own physician will also make sure he's completely recovered from the effects of this nasty bout of the flu too."

Adrian barked out a laugh that he tried his best to turn into a cough when the nurse turned her distrustful look on him.

"I'm going to have to talk to Dr. Ramirez before we can sign his discharge papers," she said.

The putative Dr. Lewis gestured toward the door. "Go ahead. I'm going to start my transfer workup with Mr. Rothschild while we wait."

The moment the nurse was out the door, he dug into the satchel bag that was looped across his body and moved toward the bed.

"Adrian, I'm Tate," he said, his voice much quieter than it had been when he'd addressed the nurse. Adrian hadn't even realized how much their voices had hurt until Tate lowered his. "Your Alpha contacted my boss a few hours ago and asked us to come extract you from the hospital."

He pulled out a pair of sweatpants and a T-shirt and handed them to Adrian.

"It'll be easier for you to walk out of here in these," Tate said.

Adrian scrambled out of the bed and grabbed the clothes, grateful Tate had planned ahead and brought him something to change into. The paramedics had cut through his button-down shirt earlier, and his pants had been taken God only knew where after he'd been admitted. The sweatpants and T-shirt were a welcome change from the backless hospital gown he'd been in.

"Do we need to run?" Adrian asked after he'd pulled the T-shirt down over his chest.

Tate threw back his head and laughed. "No. We really are waiting for Dr. Ramirez. I spoke with her before I came in, but the nurse was right to double-check the release orders. Just sit tight, and we'll have you out of here as soon as we can."

Adrian cast a worried look at the clock on the wall. It was encased in a metal cage, and the sight made him uncomfortable. Was *he* headed for a cage? Who was this Tate guy? He'd clearly talked to Adrian's mom, given the way he'd worked in the flu thing, but how did she know him? Could they really trust him, or was he just the best alternative his mom could find on such short notice?

Tate fished in his bag and came up with another clipboard, smaller than the hospital version he'd laid on the end of Adrian's bed.

"I really do have some paperwork to go through with you. Are you feeling up to it?"

Adrian gaped at him. "Paperwork?"

It came out as a croak, his throat dry. Tate reached for the Styrofoam cup of ice water on the bedside table and handed it to him, orienting the straw toward Adrian as the nurse had done when she'd helped him with it. He put a hand on Adrian's shoulder and applied gentle pressure until Adrian sat on the edge of the bed before he let him drink. Maybe this guy actually *was* a doctor?

"I'm sorry," Tate said, looking chagrined. "You must be so confused. I gather your Alpha wasn't able to give you the details?"

Adrian swallowed his drink and shook his head. "There was always someone else in the room with me."

Tate nodded. "That's standard hospital protocol when a patient comes in under a psych watch," he said. "Let me start over. I'm Tate Lewis, and I'm a psychologist who helps werewolves through the Turn."

Adrian's mind spun. "You work at one of the camps," he accused, his tone sharp.

"I do," Tate said, bobbing his head. "Camp H.O.W.L. is about an hour and half south of here in the Hoosier National Forest. Your Alpha arranged things with my director. My coworker Harris is waiting with the van. We'll be taking you back to camp where you can Turn safely."

Adrian glanced up at the clock again. It was after three. "Is there time?"

He saw Tate's Adam's apple move as he swallowed. "I certainly hope so. We're equipped to handle your Turn in the van if necessary, but I'll be honest. That wouldn't be very pleasant for you."

"Or for you," Adrian murmured softly. He'd seen half a dozen of his fellow wolflings Turn while he'd been at camp, and every single one had been a violent, painful process. The counselors had often come out of it worse for wear than the teens.

"Don't worry about us," Tate said, a bit of false cheer in his voice. "Harris and I are trained to handle it. All four of the counselors at the camp are licensed psychologists. It's a big selling point for the facility. We also have a meditation teacher, a yoga and Pilates teacher, an art therapy teacher, and a Michelin-rated chef."

"How much will that be costing me?" he asked wryly.

Tate grinned. "A lot, though you'll deal with that with the financial manager sometime next week. Your Alpha has all the paperwork and has agreed to cover the fees."

Like hell she would. Adrian wasn't going to let his mother bear the cost of what was stacking up to be the most expensive vacation he'd ever taken.

"And if I can't pay?"

"There are need-based scholarships and some grants families have made available," Tate said with a dismissive shrug. "Anne Marie—she's the director— she won't have us toss you out if you can't pay. But like I said, that's all been taken care of. Right now you just need to focus on staying calm and keeping your cool while we spring you from this place."

His words brought Adrian's attention to the way his heart was racing. He was clenching his fingers with such force his fingernails had broken the skin, so he purposefully straightened his fingers and resisted the urge to let them curl back again. Instead, he inspected the eight half-moon cuts on his palms blooming with dots of blood.

"Take a deep breath in and hold it for a few seconds," Tate said, his tone soothing and low. "Close your eyes and pick one thing to focus on. It could be the sound of my heart or maybe the ticking of the clock.

Focus on that until everything else fades away, and then let all your stress and tension go with a big exhale."

Adrian thought it sounded like new-age hooey, but he did as he was told. He bent over, hunching in on himself. The bed squeaked, making Adrian wince. But after the ringing in his ears stopped, he found he *could* hear Tate's heartbeat. It was reassuringly steady. Adrian focused on that, straining his hearing until he could even hear the whoosh of blood in the valves. He took a deep breath and blew it out slowly, and amazingly, he could actually feel himself relaxing. His shoulders dropped, his heart rate slowed, and the pins and needles that had been torturing him receded.

He opened his eyes slowly, blinking in surprise when he didn't have to flinch back because of the fluorescent lights. Tate had turned them off, leaving the room lit only by the natural light coming through the blinds-covered window. The heavy ache that had plagued Adrian's eyes faded, and he took another slow breath and sat up straight, relief running through him with such force he felt weak in the knees.

Tate crouched on the floor in front of him and met his gaze. "Better?"

"I didn't realize how keyed up I was," Adrian admitted. He felt like a teenager again—out of control and out of tune with his own body. It was ridiculous.

"It's normal. It's all part of the Turn," Tate said.

Adrian scoffed, "Nothing about my Turn is going to be normal. If I even *do* Turn."

He expected Tate to offer him some bland reassurances, but he was pleasantly surprised to see Tate nod in agreement.

"That's true. We don't know what's going to happen in your case, which makes something that was already psychologically taxing even worse. I can't imagine what it feels like to be inside your head right now. Every reaction you're having is completely valid, okay? If you're angry, if you're scared, if you're confused. There is no right or wrong way to react to Turning like this. And no matter what happens tonight after moonrise, you'll be in a safe place surrounded by people who are there to help you."

Adrian closed his eyes again and grunted. He hated psychobabble. He'd had to listen to a lot of it during the year after his non-Turn. His mother had sent him to a parade of doctors and psychologists, and each one had been just as baffled as the one before. He'd had a lot of "This isn't your fault" and "It's okay to be angry" thrown at him, and all of it had left him more furious than when he'd started. But Tate's words were different. If this guy really *was* a psychologist, he wasn't like any Adrian had worked with before. Everyone who had treated him in that disastrous year had told him how he should be feeling and accused him of suppressing his emotions. No one before Tate had ever said it was okay to not know how he was feeling.

"I'm not going to make any empty promises, Adrian," Tate said. "You're a grown man. You know how our world works. I'll do whatever I can to make things easier for you and help you through this, but it's going to fucking suck."

Adrian opened his eyes and looked at Tate in shock. Tate *was* different from the other psychologists he'd seen. "You don't pull punches, huh?"

Tate smiled, and Adrian was struck with the sudden urge to nip at the plump curve of his lower lip.

God, where had *that* come from? Tate was an attractive man, sure, but Adrian was hardly in a place to fantasize about someone. He was in the middle of his

Turn, for God's sake! This wasn't the time for his dick to go into warp drive.

Unless—could that be affected by the Turn too? It made a weird kind of sense. Everything else was hyped up to an eleven; would that apply to his libido too?

"You look troubled," Tate said, his eyes narrowing. "I thought I was doing a good job calming you down. Clearly I'm falling down on the job."

Nothing about Tate was calming any part of Adrian down right now. The smooth, sultry slide of his voice had been comforting earlier, but now it was going straight to his groin. Adrian swallowed hard and looked away, tearing his gaze from Tate's form-fitting T-shirt that molded to his biceps in the most delicious way.

Adrian shifted, uncomfortably aware his borrowed sweatpants hid nothing, and Tate cleared his throat. "Ah. Do you want me to tell you our bodies have all kinds of reactions to the Turn, or should I just stop talking?"

Damn the man for being so *nice* about this. And how the hell could Tate being decent be a turn-on? But somehow it was. The desire that had been coursing through Adrian's veins only surged hotter at the offer.

He was saved from answering by a sharp rap on the door, which swung open before he or Tate had a chance to react. Adrian scrambled back into the bed and pulled the blankets over his semihard cock.

"Looks like you're out of here, Mr. Rothschild," Dr. Ramirez said as she breezed into the room with a handful of paperwork.

## Chapter Six

"I'M just saying, I don't think giving the man a tranquilizer was necessary," Tate said with reproach.

He glanced back at Adrian, who'd made himself comfortable on the bench seat behind them before conking out on the drugs Harris had offered him.

"It was his choice," Harris said with a negligent shrug. "Sure as hell made the drive easier, didn't it?"

Tate had to give him that. Adrian had been antsy and jittery the first twenty minutes of their drive before Harris pulled into a gas station and offered him a bottle of water and a sedative. It wasn't something they'd give a teen except in the direst of circumstances, and it probably wasn't something they should be giving an adult werewolf who was Turning, since the Turn messed with body chemistry. Harris could very well have poisoned Adrian with the dose. More likely, Tate admitted grudgingly to himself, it would have simply been ineffective. He'd told Adrian both were a possibility, but Adrian had chosen to down the pills anyway. And luckily, they'd worked.

Tate was keeping a close eye on Adrian, monitoring his heart rate and his scent, which had changed subtly even over the course of the drive. He didn't think there was any chance Adrian wouldn't be fully Turning tonight. He smelled exactly like the new Turns at camp always did when they arrived. He wouldn't be sharing that with Adrian when he woke, though. The last thing Adrian needed in this situation was misinformation. Tate wasn't going to go out on a limb with his best guess—not when Adrian was so stressed.

He picked up a salty tang in the air and turned, frowning when he saw Adrian's forehead was covered with beads of sweat. He reached back and hovered his hand just over the damp skin, trying to check to see if the fever that had broken earlier had returned. That would be unusual— normally the fever signified the onset of the hormone rush, and once that started, the pain receded and didn't return. Tate didn't feel an abnormal amount of heat coming off Adrian now, so it must be another effect of the Turn.

They were about twenty minutes from camp and making good time. Moonrise wasn't until a little before seven thirty tonight, and it was just past five now. It had taken longer than he'd anticipated to get Adrian checked out of the hospital, and Harris had taken a wrong turn that had cost them a bit. Even getting on the road when they did, they'd had plenty of time. Still, Tate couldn't help but be worried. What if they got a flat? A dozen things could happen to prevent them from making it to the safety of the facility, and then how would they handle Adrian's Turn?

"I can hear you thinking from over here," Harris muttered. "He's fine. His breathing is deep and even, and his heart rate is steady. The sedative didn't do any damage. If anything, it saved his pride. He didn't want us smelling his boner all the way to Bloomington."

Tate grimaced. Adrian's arousal had been patently clear to even those without super senses, thanks to the way his erection had tented his borrowed sweatpants. It was a mental image that made Tate's own jeans grow tight, so he steered away from it. Besides, Adrian hadn't been reacting to *him*, not really. Tate had been an attractive warm body who'd been nearby while Adrian's hormones were out of control. Frankly, he could have done without knowing Adrian was attracted to men—and him in particular. It would make working together in a therapeutic relationship impossible, both because of Adrian's reaction and Tate's own attraction to him.

He'd never had this problem before. But then again, he usually treated teenagers. He'd never had to deal with a patient who was a gorgeous twenty-seven-year-old man.

"Think he'll do better with Kenya or Liam?" Tate asked, trying to keep his mind from wandering to places it shouldn't go.

Harris grunted. "That won't be our call. Anne Marie will assign him. But I'm guessing she'll give him to Kenya. She's the oldest therapist, which should help. We rely on the age gap too much, maybe."

It set them up to be an older sibling kind of mentor, which worked well for a lot of these kids. But aside from Kenya, they didn't have any therapists older than forty. Tate came in a distant second at thirty-two to her fifty-four.

"I can see that," Tate said. "His mother is his Alpha, so he should respond well to a strong female figure."

"Anne Marie will definitely give him to Kenya, then," Harris said. He pulled off onto an unmarked gravel road that took them into the Hoosier National Forest.

The camp was on private property, bordered on all sides by federal land. It was a neat trick that helped them practically disappear from maps. Tate had heard stories about a werewolf high up in the U.S. Forest Service who had negotiated similar arrangements for camps all across the country in the 1920s. Hiding the camps in plain sight was an ingenious idea.

Tate took out his cell phone and called the director to let her know they'd be there in less than ten minutes. He also updated her on Adrian's choice to take a sedative, which had led to some creative cursing on her end and a promise to have the camp doctor meet the van in the parking lot with a gurney.

"At least we won't have to carry him," Harris quipped after Tate had taken his browbeating and hung up.

"It wasn't even my idea," Tate muttered.

"You could have told him you didn't want him to do it," Harris said. "You seem to have a lot of influence with him. He's probably bonded with you."

The Turn was stressful, and like any stressful situation it tended to create a fierce trust and affection between wolflings who went through it together. Turn bonds involved an intense connection that spanned a few days and then usually receded to a normal friendship after the endorphin rush of the Turn faded. A smaller number of Turn bonds were sexual, and those tended to stick, especially if they were consummated. The staff didn't discourage either type of bond—the wolflings who came to Camp H.O.W.L. were adults, after all. But they'd never had a wolfling who'd formed a Turn bond with a counselor. And hopefully they never would, Tate thought grimly. It wouldn't be good for his own state of mind to spend too much time in close proximity to Adrian.

"As long as I'm not with him when his Turn hits full blast at moonrise, I think we'll be okay."

Harris looked over at him, his brows knitted together. "You know, having a Turn bond with you might actually help him. He's not going to bond with any of these kids, and it's hard to go it alone. There can be psychological impact from not having a Turn bondmate."

Tate was intimately acquainted with that. He'd gone through the Turn completely alone, as was the tradition with his former Pack. To say that it had been traumatic would be a huge understatement.

And if he could guarantee his Turn bond with Adrian would be platonic, that would be okay. But Tate wasn't stupid. The spike of lust in his belly when he thought about Adrian, paired with Adrian's visceral reaction to him earlier, made a platonic bond extremely unlikely. Even if they were both primed for the bond—and he was pretty sure they were—it would be inappropriate for a staffer to be involved with a camper. They had ironclad rules in place for that, and with good reason. It would be a gross misuse of power and a terrible breach of trust to take advantage of a wolfling who was fresh off their Turn, roiling with hormones and seized by their new senses and appetites.

Tate squirmed in his seat. Under no circumstances could he be Adrian's Turn bondmate.

**"IT'S** already set," Diann said with an apologetic shrug. "He's clearly tuned to you. Having you near calms his heart rate, and the sound of your voice lowers his blood pressure."

A mosquito whined near Tate's ear and he swatted at it, annoyed. There was a reason no one wandered out after dark much this time of year without fur on. His human skin was no match for the tiny menaces. He guided Diann away from the pool of light near the door, hoping the mosquitoes might not be as bad in the dark. He understood why they needed to have this conversation out of Adrian's earshot, but that didn't mean he wanted to get eaten alive while they had it.

"He was in great shape when you brought him in," Diann continued, "but his vitals have gone downhill since you dropped him off at the clinic."

Tate pursed his lips. "He was unconscious when we dropped him off, Diann. Of course his vitals were stable."

"He was awake within a minute of you leaving," she said gently. "I don't think the sedative actually had that much effect on him. With the way his metabolism is running right now, it should have burned off within half an hour. My theory is it helped him get to sleep, but then your presence kept him calm and relaxed enough to *stay* asleep. Hearing a Turn bondmate's heartbeat will do that. It's why it's important to have one."

Horror washed over Tate as he thought back to Adrian focusing on his heartbeat in the hospital room. "Could I have caused the bond if I had him zero in on my heart earlier?"

Diann chuckled. "No. It's purely chemical. Bonds only form between werewolves who are compatible— you know that. It's like biology's way of ensuring a werewolf will be safe and supported."

They were vulnerable the first time they shifted, but Turn bonds based purely on safety had stopped being commonplace after the camps had been formed. Wolflings instinctually gravitated toward older Weres who could protect them during their Turn, which was why so many families sent their wolflings to facilities like Camp H.O.W.L. Once safety was taken care of, the wolflings were free to bond for support and care—and that almost always happened with wolflings their age. Turn bonds had become about friendship instead of safety—and, in some instances, a way for Weres to find compatible mates. This was definitely not that.

"Can it be transferred?"

Diann looked at him sharply. "No. And even if it could, who would you transfer it to? One of the other wolflings? They're eight years younger than him." She shook her head. "He's already comfortable with you. Besides, would you condemn him to Turning alone?"

Only two people knew the details of his own disastrous Turn and the months that followed it before he'd been able to emancipate himself from his Pack— Diann and Kenya. And as far as Tate was concerned, it was a story he was happy never to have to tell again. It was one of the many reasons he avoided getting tangled up with other werewolves.

"I'm not comfortable bonding with him," Tate said stiffly. He couldn't believe a member of the staff was suggesting he form a Turn bond with a camper. It was against so many rules—and common decency too.

Diann leaned against the brick retaining wall that ran around the perimeter of the medical building's courtyard. "Break it down for me," she said.

"He's a camper."

"True. But he won't be assigned to you in any official capacity aside from a few of the larger lecture classes. You won't actually have any control over him. Next."

Tate ran a hand over his jaw, frustrated. "He's younger than me."

"By five years. Hardly a big deal given that you're both adults. My husband is ten years older than me. Next."

He clenched his jaw and took a deep breath in through his nose. "Turn bonds can become sexual."

She leveled him with an unimpressed look. "You poor dear. Imagine, having a consensual sexual relationship with a good-looking man."

Tate whirled on his heel and started pacing the small space. His body buzzed with caged energy—probably a direct effect of the Turn bond he and Adrian had already shared. He was feeling some of the frenzied energy that Adrian was dealing with as moonrise approached. It blended with the energy Tate already felt, unleashing something wild in him. He forced it down, his only concession his fisted hands and the pacing.

"Tate," Diann said, all teasing erased from her voice. "You're both adults. A Turn bond will only become sexual if there's mutual attraction, you know that. And if it does, well, as Doris Day sang, 'Que sera, sera.'"

He couldn't believe Diann could be so blasé when talking about a counselor entering into a sexual relationship with a camper. Even if he transferred Adrian to another psychologist, that doctor-patient relationship still existed.

"You know it's not that simple," he said. "Even if I'm not treating him here, he met me as a psychologist. *His* psychologist. I was responsible for getting him out of the hospital, something he will attach no small amount of gratitude to."

"He didn't believe you were actually a psychologist, so I wouldn't worry on that front," Diann said dryly. "Kenya did his psychological intake exam, and she agreed he'd formed no professional relationship with you. He thinks of you as the hot guy who came to drive him to camp, not as Dr. Lewis."

Tate's lips thinned. "I need to hear that from him."

Diann's laugh echoed off the brick. "Need your ego fed?"

"No, I need to know he felt attracted to me before the Turn bond started to form," he said flatly.

Her humor evaporated. "I've talked to him, and so has Kenya. We are medical professionals, Tate, just like you. We wouldn't let him be coerced into something. I don't think this is his hormones talking." She sighed and reached out to take his arm as he moved past her midpace. "This could be something special, Tate. Don't shut that out."

That probably scared Tate more than anything. He'd grown comfortable here, even though the moments he hated his job were growing more frequent. He didn't have to worry about forming attachments because most of the campers left after a month, and staffers tended not to stay much more than six months to a year. It was an in-between job. Something a werewolf at the beginning of their career would do. The exceptions were few, and all of the long-timers had a good reason not to move on. Diann had been here the longest at fifteen years. She'd lost her only son in a Turn gone wrong and dedicated her life to sparing others the same fate. Kenya only worked at the camp part-time, spending several days a week teaching classes at nearby Indiana University. She'd been there a year before she brought Tate on board. He was coming up on almost ten years himself, though a scarce few knew why he'd chosen to settle in. The next person in line was the Pilates and Soul Cycle teacher, who'd been there two. But most staffers didn't find it the kind of place where you could put down roots, which made it ideal for Tate. Roots scared him.

"I see you thinking," Diann said. "And I'm glad for it. Moonrise will be here soon. Why don't you go over to the mess hall and grab something cold to drink and a quick bite to eat? Take some time to think."

She let go of his arm and gave him a sad smile. "If you decide you don't want to do it, we'll manage. Don't come back to the infirmary if you don't intend to stay. It will be easier for Adrian not to have you there at all if you aren't going to honor the Turn bond."

That stung, but it was fair. Tate hadn't been aware they were forming the bond, but there must have been something in the kind of signals he was putting out that made Adrian's subconscious latch on. It wasn't either of their faults—it just *was.* And now he was going to have to figure out whether or not he could handle it.

## Chapter Seven

**ADRIAN** had always considered himself to be an articulate person, so he was surprised to find himself at a loss for words to describe how he was feeling. His senses were in overdrive, and he was so hyperaware of everything around him he felt like he might burst. He couldn't concentrate on anything Kenya was saying because he kept getting distracted by things happening in other parts of the infirmary.

"Your body knows what to do," Kenya said, and Adrian's attention snapped back to her. "Trust your instincts."

His instincts were telling him to tear out of the building and go after his Turn bondmate, but Adrian knew that would be a mistake. He'd heard every word of Tate and Diann's conversation in the courtyard, and he had to wonder if that had been intentional. She'd said his hearing was abnormally acute, which made him think most of the wolflings wouldn't have been able to hear them. But nothing about Adrian's Turn was going to be normal, it seemed. When Diann had come back in to check his vitals after Tate left, she'd given him a very odd, appraising look. Had she been silently judging his reaction? What did they expect him to do? Chase after Tate like an animal?

As much as he'd like to do just that, Adrian wasn't going to debase himself—or Tate—that way. He'd read about Turn bonds years ago. He'd even hoped for one, naively sizing up his fellow campers as the hours crept closer to the full moon, wondering which one of them might be the one to bond with him so they could help each other through the Turn.

It was silly, of course. Not everyone formed a bond, and most of the bonds that formed were platonic. That hadn't stopped a nineteen-year-old Adrian from hoping, fantasizing even, about what it would be like to have a bond. Ironic because now that he had one, he'd give just about anything to get rid of it. Not for himself, but for Tate. Adrian didn't mind—quite the contrary. It was pleasant and soothing for him. Tate's presence was like slipping into a warm bath or cozying up to a fire on a cold day. Tate seemed to radiate calmness and Adrian's own body was powerless to do anything but relax.

He'd found it hard to believe he'd only slept an hour in the van. Aside from the crick in his neck from his head resting against the window, Adrian woke feeling more rested than he had in weeks. Dr. Roget, who'd insisted Adrian call her Diann, had explained that was because of Tate's presence.

He'd ease the Turn too, if they spent it together. It would still be painful, but not to the degree it would be going it alone. Adrian would Turn faster, shift easier, and come back to his senses faster with Tate there than he would on his own. With any luck, he wouldn't experience bloodlust at all.

*If* Tate came back. But it was selfish to hope he would, so Adrian tried hard not to wish for it. Tate had sounded wrecked over the bond, and being responsible for putting that resignation in his voice made Adrian's stomach sink. If there were a way to release Tate, Adrian would have done it as soon as Tate had voiced his reluctance to Diann.

But he couldn't, and fighting the Turn bond wouldn't do any good. It could quite possibly make the Turn even harder, or so Kenya had told him. It was strange—no one here seemed to rest on formality, which was odd given that werewolf culture was all about hierarchy. But Kenya—Dr. Marcus, according to her badge—had told him to call her by her first name, like Diann had. He wondered if it was his age or if all the campers did. It was so different from the Pack hierarchy at home. His mother would shit a brick if one of her Weres called her by her first name.

Kenya cleared her throat, and Adrian shifted his gaze from the empty doorway to her face. She had laugh lines and the deepest dimples he'd ever seen. Looking at her made Adrian want to be happy, no matter how impossible that was right now.

"We have rooms set up downstairs for the campers to Turn in," she said gently, "but I thought you'd be more comfortable in the isolation room."

Adrian cast one last look at the door and closed his eyes. He'd be doing this alone, then.

"No one is left alone," Kenya murmured, causing Adrian to wonder if he'd voiced his last thought. She smiled. "It's a common fear. But don't worry. The purpose of the special rooms is to make wolflings more comfortable, not because we are going to lock you in and leave you to face the moon by yourself."

Adrian followed her downstairs, entering through a hidden pocket door in Diann's office. "The basement isn't on any official blueprints," Kenya explained as they made their way down the well-lit staircase. It was glazed concrete that looked every bit as modern and well cared for as the infirmary itself had been. "That way when human officials come to inspect the camp we don't have to worry about them stumbling on this."

She pushed open a door at the bottom of the stairs, and Adrian gaped at the expansive area revealed. This room alone had to be bigger than the entire footprint of the infirmary above, and there were corridors and doors heading in all directions. The place was huge.

"It runs under most of the buildings that form the center of the camp," Kenya explained. "All of those buildings have hidden entrances."

At least a dozen wolflings milled around the large room, each looking as antsy as he felt. Adults he assumed were counselors like Tate roamed around too, having quiet words with the campers who looked the most distressed.

"We don't have enough counselors for a one-to-one ratio, but you'll be the exception," she said, her tone apologetic.

Adrian didn't need to ask why. She said the isolation room was to make him more comfortable, but the truth was no one knew how he was going to handle the Turn, given his advanced age and quirky biology.

He didn't blame them for taking measures to keep the other campers safe.

"The counselors each have a core group of campers they advise and mentor," Kenya said. "They aren't usually the counselor assigned to monitor the camper's bunkhouse, so each camper has at least two counselors they're comfortable with. We'll split them off in small groups here in a bit."

Adrian tried for a smile but knew he'd failed miserably when Kenya reached out and patted his shoulder. "Diann will be with you," she said. "I've got a group myself, or I'd volunteer to stay with you as well."

Guilt tugged at Adrian's stomach. He didn't want to pull resources away from the wolflings. He was a grown man, for God's sake. He could do this by himself. It would probably be better, even. That way there wouldn't be anyone there to witness all the indignities of the Turn. No one needed to see him like that.

He pasted on his best reassuring smile. "I don't need—"

"I'll be with him," Tate said from behind them, and Adrian's entire body went on high alert, tingling with awareness. Goose bumps cascaded over his skin, and every nerve sang.

Tate closed the distance between them and put a warm hand between Adrian's shoulder blades. Muscles he hadn't even realized had been knotted with anxiety and fear unclenched, and Adrian would have sworn he grew an inch taller from the weight that fell off his shoulders. He leaned into the touch like a plant growing toward the light, seeking more.

Tate leaned in closer, his breath ghosting along the shell of Adrian's ear. "That is, assuming you want me there."

Adrian nearly choked in his rush to respond. It was like he'd forgotten how to swallow. Coughing, he ducked his chin in embarrassment. "Yes," he managed to croak.

Tate's low chuckle turned Adrian's bones to putty. He sagged back against Tate's body, but Tate seemed to have anticipated Adrian's weight, because he was already braced for it. His only reaction was a brief huff of air at the sudden impact.

Adrian looked up when Kenya clucked her tongue. "You're going to have to do better than that," she said, her dark eyes moving from Adrian to Tate. "Moonrise will be here soon, so you'd better get whatever you want out of him before that happens, Tate. He won't be able to enter into any provisos when he's taken by the Turn."

Adrian's spirits sank. Of course Tate would be doing this for some ulterior motive. Would he want money? Or maybe the kind of influence Adrian's Pack could provide? The werewolf world was governed by power plays like this one, but he'd been naive enough to hope Tate had agreed because he too felt the tug of the bond.

Not every Turn bond was sexual—most were platonic, actually—but Adrian had hoped theirs would be one of the bonds that ended in more. His mother and father had been Turn bondmates, and their chemistry had been so great they'd spun the simple bond into something much deeper. He'd always wanted something like that, and when he hadn't Turned, Adrian had written it off as a fairy tale. He gave up his fantasies of having a Turn bond, and the tiny part of him that had hoped for something truly rare, a special bond that was more than platonic, died as well. But here he was, falling into that trap again. He should know better. A werewolf of all people should know how badly fairy tales usually ended.

Kenya gave both of them a stern look before hurrying off to a small group of wolflings who had started fighting at the edge of the room. Adrian looked up, surprised to see it had mostly emptied out. Kenya had been right—moonrise was upon them. He could feel it tugging at his bones like the satisfaction of a well-deserved stretch.

But his stomach was also churning and his skin prickling painfully, and those sensations were so at odds with the pleasurable twinge in his bones that he hardly knew what was what.

"There are smaller rooms down the corridor," Tate said. He started moving, and Adrian was surprised to find himself moving too. His body was already finely tuned to Tate's. All it took was the slightest nudge from the hand that lingered on Adrian's back and he was moving in the direction Tate had set them.

Adrian's body was buzzing now, an itch creeping deep into his flesh that made him want to tear at his skin. Intellectually he knew it would pass, but it was hard to remember that in the moment. This was another reason werewolves didn't go through the Turn alone—they could tear themselves apart if they had to face the pain and fear by themselves.

"Here we are," Tate said, removing his hand from Adrian's back to open a door at the end of the corridor. He held it open with his hip and reached inside to turn the lights on. Adrian ached at the loss of contact, but it was brief. Tate reached for him and lightly stroked Adrian's neck with the rough pads of his fingers. Adrian relaxed instantly, leaning into the touch, and

Tate let out a quiet sigh and palmed his nape, squeezing it lightly.

Unlike the corridor and the large room they'd been in, there were no overhead fluorescent lights in the room Tate had brought him to. Sconces on the wall glowed softly, illuminating the room without stinging Adrian's sensitive eyes. He stepped inside reluctantly. Once the door closed behind them, the Turn would be real. Not that it wasn't now—his aching joints and tortured skin were plenty real—but officially being in a Turning room made it so much more serious.

He swallowed hard as the door clicked shut behind Tate, relieved when there was no snick of a lock. He could leave if he wanted to. It would be unwise, and if Tate was a Turn bondmate worth his salt, he would heavily discourage it, but Adrian wasn't trapped. His pulse slowed a bit at the knowledge that he wasn't being locked up.

"Moonrise is in about fifteen minutes," Tate said, his eyes crinkling in sympathy when Adrian winced. "I'm sorry I didn't come get you earlier. We should have had you settled into the room a while ago."

That would only have prolonged the growing sense of dread forming in Adrian's stomach, and he said as much.

"I'm not going to lie—the Turn is painful," Tate said, a small, sad smile twisting his lips. "And unfortunately there isn't much I can do to ease that. But this is a safe place for you. You won't be able to damage anything important here."

Adrian looked around the room. He skipped his gaze over the bed in the corner quickly, not wanting to think about that. There were no windows, of course, being in the basement, but there were paintings on the walls and a door slightly ajar at the far end. A bathroom, he presumed, catching a glance of a sink. The floor in the corridor was concrete, but the room had rubbery linoleum-type flooring that felt almost spongy beneath his feet. The center of the room was covered with a large, plush-looking rug, and there was an overstuffed armchair and a bookcase full of reading material next to it.

"There may be periods between you shifting and being zonked out when you're lucid and awake," Tate explained with a shrug. "Plus it gets boring for whoever's in here with you, believe it or not."

Adrian could have used a bookshelf full of novels and magazines when he'd waited all night without Turning.

"Could you just drug a wolfling so they slept through it?"

"They've tried that. It didn't work." Tate offered Adrian his hand. "The only thing that can help prevent a wolfling from falling into bloodlust during the Turn is having a bond. We're getting close now. Can you feel it?"

Adrian's heart thudded at the reminder, despite the fact that his body was essentially a walking countdown to moonrise. He knew they had less than five minutes left. He couldn't put how he knew into words, but he did. He could literally *feel* the moon.

"Before you give in to the pull, I need to talk to you," Tate said.

Adrian nodded, wary. Was this where Tate asked for favors? Made demands? Adrian was hardly in a position to turn him down, whatever they were.

"This is unusual, having a Turn bond between a staff member and a camper. And I'm not going to lie,

I'm attracted to you. It's going to make it difficult not to give in if the bond turns sexual. I promise you I'll do my best not to take advantage of you, but I need to know if you consent. I need to know what you're okay with, Adrian."

Adrian blinked. *That* was what Tate wanted? Consent? "Yes," he mumbled.

"No." Tate's voice was firm. "That's not enough. I need to know if you accept the Turn bond and the possibility that ours might not be platonic."

Laughter bubbled up in Adrian's chest. He felt giddy and lightheaded. "Yes," he said, grimacing when his voice cracked. "I consent. To the bond. To everything."

Tate studied him solemnly for a moment before nodding. "Good enough. But I was serious about not taking advantage of you. I'll do my best, Adrian. You have my word."

Adrian didn't want his word on that. He'd rather let the bond go where it wanted—especially if it meant getting to take Tate to bed. But he understood how hard this had to be for someone like Tate who'd spent his career protecting wolflings.

"'Kay," he slurred. He sank down onto the bed, looking for any relief for his aching body.

His head was beginning to feel fuzzy. Tate's voice sounded faraway, like he was speaking to Adrian through a tunnel. His arm didn't hurt anymore, but his entire body felt like it was made of stone. His head bobbed forward, too heavy for his neck to hold.

"Here we go," Tate said, drawing out the first word. "Welcome, moonrise."

He grasped Adrian under the arms and hauled him off the bed and onto the rug that had looked so soft earlier. "You don't want to be up there for this, trust me. You're going to end up on the floor one way or another, and if you start down here there will be fewer bruises later."

Adrian pressed his face into the rug. He was sure he could feel each and every fiber, but he didn't open his eyes to see if he could count them. He couldn't have opened his lids if he'd wanted to—they felt like they were welded shut.

"Let the Turn happen," Tate crooned in his faraway voice. His hand cupped the back of Adrian's neck, but instead of being comforting like it had been earlier, it rasped against his skin like sandpaper. Adrian wiggled away. Or tried to, at least. In reality he didn't make it far. Maybe a few carpet fibers away. They dragged against his cheek, irritating his skin.

Tate moved his hand from Adrian's neck to his hair, his fingers stroking softly. It felt good, and Adrian tried to arch a bit into the touch but instead found himself unable to stop. His back bent harshly, raising his stomach and face up off the carpet. He felt like his bones might snap under the pressure.

Tate's gentle touch disappeared, and Adrian tried to protest but couldn't get words out past molasses-thick saliva. His tongue pressed against his teeth with such force they ached.

"Shhhhh." Tate's voice was closer, and Adrian managed to force one eye open, surprised to see that Tate had lain on his side next to Adrian on the carpet, their faces inches apart. "It's worse if you fight it. Try to relax your muscles so they won't strain so much."

Try to *relax*? Was Tate kidding? Adrian was sure his bones were shattering. Jagged points pressed against his skin, shredding muscle and sinew in their quest to escape his body.

With great effort he managed to gain control of his tongue so he could speak. "Fuck. You," he rasped.

Anger licked through him, hot and sharp, when Tate laughed. Adrian clenched his hands, shocked to find his fingernails had grown into talon-like daggers that parted the flesh of his palm like butter. The pain barely registered—it was a blip in the sea of agony that washed over him. A welcome relief, almost, to find one area to focus on instead of the haze of pain that had settled over every inch of his body.

"You're doing so well," Tate said, his voice clearer than it had been a minute ago. He hadn't moved, so it must be Adrian's hearing coming back. He rubbed his face against the carpet, finding he could no longer differentiate each fiber. His senses were normalizing. Surely the pain would settle soon after, wouldn't it?

It would have to. Adrian couldn't imagine keeping up with this kind of white-hot agony for much longer. He tried to focus past the pain and think about something else, but his world had narrowed to the strip of carpet he was currently dying on and Tate's voice, which had continued to croon encouragement as Adrian slipped in and out of lucidity.

Another spasm overtook Adrian, fire lancing down his bent back and pooling at the base of his spine. His hips snapped and his knees fused, the blood in his legs replaced with lava as the Turn coursed through him.

Adrian's pain had given him a surge of strength, but it ebbed as quickly as it had come. He collapsed onto the rug, his limbs caught underneath him and his nose squashed into the pile. He needed to turn his head to breathe, but at the moment he didn't have the energy.

Tate's hands were blessedly cool against Adrian's face as he tilted his head to the side. They'd felt like sandpaper before, but now the touch was as refreshing and soothing as silk.

"Rest up a bit," Tate said. "Do you want me to help you sit up so you can have a drink of water?"

Adrian's eyes flew open in panic. "No," he moaned. He never wanted to be upright again. He wanted to live out the rest of his life on this floor. It was a nice floor. Flat. Supportive.

"Okay, okay."

Adrian closed his eyes for just a moment, and then opened them in shock when something cold and wet wiped over his forehead. He blinked hard when water ran into his eyes. Tate had a washcloth. When had he gotten a washcloth?

"You slept for about an hour," Tate said. "Your muscles started twitching and spasming again a few minutes ago, which is why I woke you. The shift will be coming on soon. Get yourself ready."

He dabbed the cloth over Adrian's neck and chest, and Adrian looked down. He wasn't wearing a shirt. That wasn't right, was it? He'd been fully dressed when all this started.

"I undressed you while you were conked out," Tate explained, shrugging slightly when Adrian narrowed his eyes. "You're probably sore as hell already. I didn't think you'd want to be awake for it. It's going to feel like you were hit by a Mack truck for a few days. Lifting your arms above your head will make you want to weep. So I took advantage of your unconsciousness and got you ready for the shift."

Right. The part of the night where Adrian's Turn would finish and his body would reshape itself into a wolf's. Well, not a wolf's. His. But him as a wolf. It was too much to wrap his aching head around. He'd been young and excited last time around and not very prone to navel-gazing. But coming into this as an adult—it was big. He didn't know how to describe the combination of excitement and fear warring inside him. His body was literally going to be changing shape. That was awesome. It was going to be doing it whether he wanted it to or not, completely outside his control. That was *not* awesome.

Maybe teenagers felt the loss of control less keenly because they'd never really had much control over their lives. But Adrian was an adult. He separated his whites and colors. He ate quinoa. He paid his taxes. He had an IRA. He didn't relish the idea of not being in control of his body, even if it was just for the initial shift.

Tate stopped the impromptu sponge bath and sat back on his heels, watching Adrian with concern. Adrian was momentarily confused by it, but then realized Tate was probably expecting him to respond.

His mouth was like the Sahara, but he licked at his lips and spoke. "Thanks."

Tate's tense expression eased, and he nodded. "Let's get some water in you. You weren't interested in it before your nap, but you've been sweating like crazy, and I'm worried about your hydration level."

Adrian groaned but took the hand Tate stretched out to him, unapologetically letting Tate exert all the energy necessary to pull him into a sitting position. He started to slump the minute Tate eased back, but Tate seemed to have planned for that. He slipped around behind Adrian and let Adrian lean against the solid, warm wall of his chest, one arm wrapped around Adrian's shoulders to hold him in place.

Adrian's arms trembled when he tried to take the bottle of water Tate offered him, and Tate changed course and held the bottle up to Adrian's lips, bracing it while Adrian took a careful sip. His head wasn't pounding anymore, but he'd traded the migraine for a roiling stomach. When the first sip didn't immediately come back up, he guzzled at the bottle greedily, letting the cold liquid soothe his dry throat.

Tate only let him have about half the bottle before he pulled it back. Adrian made a small sound of disappointment and then winced—he sounded like a wounded cat.

"You can have as much water as you want after the next part, okay? Trust me, you don't want to shift with a stomach full of liquid."

That sounded ominous, but Adrian was too tired to ask Tate to expound on it. It sounded like a good story, and he hoped he'd remember to ask about it later. For now, he had all he could do to remain upright, even with Tate's help.

Tate leaned in and spoke softly, his breath playing against the curve of Adrian's ear. "The worst is past, I promise."

"Unlikely," Adrian said, pleased his voice was much stronger than it had been when he'd woken. Less like a dying cat; more like an angry toad.

Tate hummed noncommittally, and Adrian nestled closer to him, the warmth of Tate's broad chest soothing the aching muscles in his back and neck. Sweat had broken out across Adrian's upper lip and brow, itchy and annoying. His arms were so weak he couldn't raise his hands to swipe it away, so he left it.

"It's true," Tate insisted. "Your first shift will hurt, but I guarantee it won't be like the pain of the Turn. Your body is primed for this now. And once you've gotten it down, shifting won't hurt. Honestly, I think a lot of the pain wolflings experience with their first dozen or so shifts is psychological. It *should* hurt. Your bones and muscles are breaking and knitting themselves back together in a new configuration. Everything we know about our bodies says that should be agonizing."

Adrian huffed. "It should hurt, so it does?" He flexed his shoulders, trying to ease the crick in his neck. "Does a wolfling in a box exist as both a wolf and a human until you can open the box to prove otherwise?"

Tate brought his fingers to Adrian's neck and honed in on the knot giving him grief. Adrian went boneless at the touch.

"Schrödinger's Werewolf? I like it."

Tate's approval brought a pleased smile to Adrian's lips, but it melted away when the first spasm of the shift hit.

"I think it's happening," he gasped as a spasm hard enough to break bone hit him.

His awareness sank inward until all he could hear was his own too-quick heartbeat and the sound of his body breaking and remaking itself. For the first time since the Turn started, he screamed.

## *Chapter Eight*

**TATE** eased Adrian's contorted body onto the rug and scooted across the floor until his back hit the wall. Adrian would be pissed at him for lying about the shift—or at least lying about how much it would hurt—when he was himself again, but he would deal with the fallout from that when it came. Going into the shift tensed up made it hurt worse, so his white lie served a purpose. Adrian had been relaxed when the shift began, and that would mean a quicker recovery and less soreness when it was over.

It did get better. Tate's shift was seamless now, a blink-and-you'd-miss-it affair he could execute at will. It still hurt, but it wasn't the drawn-out, agonizing torture Adrian and all the other wolflings who were shifting tonight were going through. Control came with practice and time, and a lot of that was governed by the werewolf's psyche. That hadn't been a lie either.

He chuckled to himself as he thought about Adrian's Schrödinger joke. If Adrian could come up with something like that while he was strung out and pain drunk during the Turn, he must really be something when he was firing on all cylinders. Part of Tate hoped he'd get a chance to find out, but another part of him, the part he hid away and tried not to indulge, worried someone like Adrian would be too perceptive. There were things in Tate's past that needed to remain buried, and Adrian was the kind of guy who could cause Tate's carefully constructed life to unravel.

He wouldn't let it get that far. No matter what Diann said, he was doing fine. Accepting that he had a Turn bond with Adrian was as far over the line as he was going to go. It meant they were compatible but it didn't have to mean anything more. He'd get Adrian through tonight, and then he'd distance himself. Kenya would be Adrian's counselor, and he could share a room with Harris.

Adrian let out an anguished groan and curled into a ball on the carpet, and the wall Tate had spent the evening trying to build crumbled. He could never bear to see anyone in pain, but it was worse with Adrian. He *felt* it. Deep in his gut, old wounds he'd blocked out years ago welled fresh metaphorical blood. Adrian's shift was turning them both inside out.

Tate kept his distance even though he wanted to crouch on the carpet and take Adrian in his arms. It wouldn't do any good—at this stage of the Turn, Adrian was past outside intervention. His body had prepared itself for the shift, and now it was happening.

Either Adrian would fully shift into his wolf form or he'd die trying.

It didn't happen often—fatalities were rare, and they were almost always brought on by external sources. Unsecured furniture crashing down. Hypothermia from shifting outside. Wolflings left on their own in the mindless throes of bloodlust.

Tate shivered and immediately cursed himself. That wasn't going to happen with Adrian. He was in a safe place, and he had Tate. It was nothing like Tate's own Turn, and the less he thought about it the better. It didn't do any good to dwell on old memories, and it certainly wasn't going to help Adrian if Tate was wallowing in self-pity.

He watched Adrian writhe and twitch on the floor with an almost clinical eye. Probably another ten minutes. Twenty tops. And then it would be done. Adrian would have attained his wolf form, and he'd probably be exhausted and pass out for a few hours before the onset of dawn brought his shift to an end and he went through the process in reverse.

That's how it almost always was for wolflings. Technically they could shift at will, but inexperience and fear usually prevented them from trying to shift back to human form before the moon set. Fear often led to aggression, which was another danger for shifted wolflings. It was why werewolves had developed the camp system years ago. Having wolflings in a place primed for their uncontrolled shifts with trained werewolves who could help them was best for everyone. They could do serious harm to themselves and others around them otherwise.

The trauma of the initial frenzy faded over time, just like any sense memory did. As the horror of the pain and terror from the initial Turn became less clear, exerting control over the shift became easier. Kenya called it leaning into the pain, treating it like an old friend rather than an enemy. Tate had never seen it that way, but rather as something that had to be borne. Both philosophies worked—whatever got a werewolf through the mental block.

Adrian's Turn was one of the most extreme Tate had ever seen. It made sense. Teenagers were still pliant and unformed—an adult's bones were done growing, their tendons and ligaments unaccustomed to the stretch of growth spurts that could add on inches in weeks. Adrian's adult body was out of practice at the transformation game, and he'd suffered mightily for it. The only saving grace here was that Adrian had passed out.

Tate moved to the bathroom to grab a towel, then hesitated and doubled back to grab a stack of them. He needed one to clean up the bowl of water Adrian had sent flying when his legs had spasmed, and it would be good to have some on hand just in case Adrian came back to himself again tonight. Tate sopped up the mess on the floor and tossed the wet towel into the sink in the bathroom to deal with later. He didn't like the idea of Adrian being out of his sight, which was ridiculous. He was four feet away—Tate would know instantly if something was wrong. But there was a tightening in his chest and a vibration in his bones that felt plain *wrong* whenever he wasn't within touching distance of Adrian.

Probably the Turn bond's way of making sure the bondee took good care of the wolfling, he figured. Though that didn't account for the way Tate's heart quickened every time the Turn eased and Adrian's face slackened in relief. He was the most beautiful man Tate had ever seen, and that wasn't just his dry spell talking. He was surrounded by teenagers here, and there hadn't been a lot of fine specimens in his native rural Idaho. He'd been too raw in college to spend much energy looking at guys, and too self-conscious to pursue any who looked like Adrian.

No one likes a psychologist having a pity party, he reminded himself. And boy, could he throw a good one. It had balloons, party hats, and all the hallmarks of an abusive childhood. PTSD, attachment disorder, anxiety—he was a walking embodiment of the DSM, the holy grail of psychology texts.

Adrian sat up suddenly, his eyes flying open. Tate lunged forward to grab him as Adrian collapsed just as quickly. Tate managed to cushion his fall with his own body, then cursed himself when he realized the dangerous situation he'd put himself in. Adrian was on the cusp of shifting, and even with the benefit of the drugs, he would be wild with pain and confusion for the shift. Tate had just trapped himself beneath a one-hundred-and-eighty-pound man who was about to sprout lethal claws and teeth for the first time in his life.

Before Tate could wedge himself out from underneath Adrian's dead weight, Adrian let out a guttural scream and started to change. Moving now would just increase the likelihood of getting hurt, so Tate wiggled an arm up to shield his face, closed his eyes, and hoped for the best.

He could feel Adrian's form changing. Coarse fur bristled where smooth, hot skin had been a moment before. Limbs shortened and bent, and Tate struggled for breath when Adrian's weight concentrated over his chest.

Tate fought to stay calm. Even if he wasn't in control of himself, Adrian would subconsciously take cues from Tate through their Turn bond. If Tate's heart rate was out of control, Adrian would sense that and go on the alert for danger, not realizing *he* was the danger. Tate drew a deep, slow breath in as best he could manage with Adrian's weight over his lungs. He held it for a few beats and blew it out through his nose. His body started to respond, settling the fight-or-flight response that had been blaring through him.

Should he move Adrian? It had been a few minutes since Tate felt him so much as twitch, so it was possible he'd passed out again from shock or exhaustion. Tate blinked one eye open and looked down. Adrian had attained his wolf form, and just as Tate had thought, he was curled up on Tate's chest, asleep.

It was best not to touch a recent Turn, but Tate couldn't maintain this position. He moved the arm that had been protecting his face, inching it down his body to brace against the floor so he could attempt to dislodge Adrian's sleeping form.

A growl split the air before Tate even straightened his elbow. Shit.

Tate looked down and came eye-to-eye with the wolf, eliciting another low warning growl.

Double shit.

He was trained for this kind of situation. He did this for a living. He knew *exactly what to do* when he came across a newly shifted wolfling while in human form himself.

And he'd already broken the first, most basic, most important rule. *Don't make eye contact.*

They weren't wolves, despite the resemblance when they were in shifted form. They looked like a wolf's larger cousin. Identical except for size, because even the magic of the shift couldn't erase body mass. If you were a one-hundred-and-eighty-pound man, you'd be a one-hundred-and-eighty-pound wolf.

And usually they retained their sense of self, their thoughts, their memories—everything that made a person *himself*—when they shifted. Unless they had succumbed to moon madness or were newly Turned. In those cases, werewolves acted on base instinct similar to a regular wolf's. Anyone they encountered was either prey or an enemy. And by making eye contact, Tate had just labeled himself the latter.

He immediately averted his eyes, but the damage had been done. Adrian shot to his feet, standing clumsily and bringing his muzzle close to Tate's face. Tate didn't move a muscle, letting Adrian scent him and assert his dominance.

If Tate had been in wolf form himself, Adrian's wolf would have recognized him as an elder and deferred to him. But it was too late for him to risk a shift, and it would only make Adrian even more aggressive.

Tate's lungs burned, but he didn't dare breathe. He didn't want to give Adrian any reason to think he was a threat.

Finally, Adrian stepped back, and Tate took in a ragged breath that made him dizzy with relief. He could feel bruises forming where Adrian's forelegs had been standing on his chest, but he didn't try to rub away the sting. He simply lay there, his muscles tensed, limbs itching with the need to move, to run.

He couldn't control his flinch when Adrian reared forward and stuck his nose against Tate's throat. His horror quickly turned to shock at the movement when Adrian raised his muzzle, using it to lift Tate's face.

Tate complied, baffled, and then watched as Adrian carefully lifted his own head and exposed his neck to Tate.

All the air in Tate's lungs left him in a rush, and he scrambled to sit up. Adrian was offering him a promise he wouldn't hurt Tate.

He'd never seen an agitated new Turn act like this. Tate had been braced—rightly so, because he was the one who'd done the wrong thing—for an attack. That he was getting out of this with no more than Adrian's hot breath on his cheek was amazing. A miracle.

The Turn bond, his mind supplied. This was the bond. Tate stood on shaky legs and backed away, not willing to risk showing his back despite Adrian's actions. He seemed lucid, but that didn't mean he couldn't turn on Tate in a heartbeat. Tate retreated until he felt a solid wall against his back. Only then did he let himself really *look* at Adrian.

He had coltish long legs, like Adrian did in human form, and a thick coat of fur that would start to shed on Adrian's first shift outdoors, once his body realized there was no need for the insulation of the downy underfur in the ninety-degree heat of an Indiana summer. His top coat was so dark it was almost black, a shade different from Adrian's rich brunet human hair. He didn't have much variation in his coloring, which was abnormal. Tate wondered what Adrian's family looked like when they shifted. Did they all have such lustrous, gorgeously hued fur, or was this yet another way Adrian was different?

Tate himself had tawny, dirty-looking fur that faded to off-white near his belly. He'd never cared about what he looked like shifted before, but a wave of shame passed over him as he took in Adrian's form. As a human and a wolf, Adrian was way out of his league. This Turn bond was some sort of cosmic joke.

He shook away the ridiculous thoughts and tried to regain some semblance of control over the situation. "Are you thirsty?" he asked Adrian, who cocked his head in response but didn't move.

"Do you want to take a nap? The bed is comfy," Tate offered, but again there was no movement across the room. Adrian was taking everything in through solemn, dark eyes, but he gave Tate no clues about what he wanted.

"I don't have any food you'd like right now," Tate tried. "Just some power bars and trail mix. Eating will have to wait until you've shifted back, I'm afraid."

Adrian's head shot up and he bounded across the room, taking Tate by surprise. Tate pressed himself up against the wall, waiting for an attack that never came. Adrian stopped a hair's breadth away and sat on his haunches, his gaze expectant.

"Food?" Tate asked breathlessly.

Nothing.

He chewed on his lip for a moment, unsure of what to do next, when it hit him. "You want to shift?"

Adrian let out a sharp, loud bark.

"This is a little bit too much like *Lassie*," Tate muttered to himself. He'd never tried to communicate with a werewolf in shifted form while he himself was human before. And when he was running with a group of shifted werewolves, there wasn't any reason to try to communicate. Their sensitive noses were able to navigate most situations for them. Fear, happiness, pain, hunger, thirst—almost every strong emotion or feeling had a scent. The same was true in human form, but their noses were less streamlined to pick it up then.

An emotion had to be very strong for Tate to be able to scent it out as a human, but he could pick up the anxiety coming off Adrian in waves now that he was so close and Tate's senses weren't overwhelmed by his own panic.

"Okay," he said, releasing a long breath. "You want to shift back."

Adrian shifted his paws slightly, like he was digging in and getting ready for something.

"It's not—it's not something you can force," Tate said, and Adrian's shoulders dipped a bit.

God, he was botching everything. This was literally his job. He'd helped hundreds of wolflings through this exact thing. If Adrian hadn't formed a Turn bond with him, Tate would be in a room with three wolflings monitoring their shift right now. And he'd be handling that a hundred times better than he was handling Adrian.

He tried to shove his emotions out of the way, imagining putting them in a box and setting it to the side like he did when he was going into counseling sessions. He needed to be a blank canvas, in control of himself and open to helping Adrian. Images from his own Turn kept flashing through his head, unbidden. It wasn't helping.

Tate slid down the wall and settled on the floor next to Adrian. "Do you mind if I touch you?" he asked, his hand hovering a few inches above Adrian's coat.

Adrian ducked his head and brought it up under Tate's outstretched arm, nudging it. Tate took the invitation for what it was and cupped his hand around the top of Adrian's skull, fingers slipping into the soft, dense fur. Adrian visibly relaxed at the touch, just as Tate had intended.

"Shifting—either to wolf form or to human form—is a natural function for us. If you think about it too much, it will be difficult." Tate explained, his own stress levels responding to having his hands in Adrian's fur. "Like breathing. We just do it, right? Naturally. It requires literally no thought. We don't have this constant internal monologue about how we need to take another breath, right? Our bodies just do it. In fact, when you *do* think about it, it becomes harder. The shift is a lot like that. Our lungs need oxygen, so we breathe. The shift happens because we need it to. Your body needs to become human, so the shift takes over and does it for you."

He stroked his hand lower, fingers running between Adrian's shoulder blades. "The shift isn't a conscious thing. We don't think, 'Okay, now I'm going to have claws.' It just happens. So try to relax. If you want to stay like this for the night, that's fine. The moonset will force your shift, like the moonrise did. But if you want your human form right now, you can shift on your own. Just think about being human, relax, and let it happen."

Adrian was still for a moment. A low, sad whine came from his throat, and Tate couldn't help but chuckle. "It's harder than it sounds," he admitted. "But not impossible, I promise."

Adrian whined again, sharper this time. Tate paused his petting until Adrian nudged his chest with his nose.

"Oh, right. I guess promises from me won't be worth much to you now," he said as he resumed his slow massage down Adrian's back. "But aren't you glad I lied? Did you *want* me to tell you it would be the most painful thing you'd ever experienced?"

Adrian growled, short and low.

"Right? Better to have gone into it not expecting it," Tate said. "Really, though, I'm not lying. Once you get control of your shift, you can do it at will. I mean, I'm human right now, aren't I? That wouldn't be possible if I didn't have control over my shift."

He felt the pull of the moon, but it was more like a suggestion, not a command. It would take at least a few weeks before Adrian had that kind of control. Most mastered it before their second full moon, but not all wolflings did.

Tate thought about Ryan. He was supposed to be with Tate tonight. With a month of training under his belt, his night should have been easier for him than for his fellow wolflings who were in the throes of their Turn, but with his dicey control, his shift would be as forced as theirs. Who had ended up with him tonight? Probably Harris. Hopefully they were working on the same thing he and Adrian were right now.

Adrian had gone still and closed his eyes, fur bristling and body almost vibrating with how intensely he was straining. Tate didn't intervene, even though he was certain it wouldn't work. After a moment, Adrian whined and pawed at his muzzle, obviously distressed by his failure.

"Just take a few deep breaths," Tate said, pitching his voice a bit lower to try to keep it soothing. "Maybe think about how different that feels in this form. Have you noticed that?"

Adrian probably hadn't, but Tate knew talking about it would make him focus on it. Noticing the little things would help push Adrian out of his mind a bit and make it easier for his body to follow its instincts and shift.

"Take in some breaths and think about how different that feels in the body you're in right now. The air doesn't taste the same, does it? How does it feel when you breathe? Draw a breath in through your nose and fill your lungs. Your chest expands differently in this form than it does when you're a human. Use that feeling. Remember what it feels like as a human, and on your next big breath in, focus on how you'd expect it to feel if you were a person, not a wolf."

Tate had to force himself not to stroke Adrian's fur while he was concentrating. He wanted to bury his hands in the coarse fur again, but Adrian needed to be able to focus on his shift—that meant no extra sensory inputs. So Tate kept his hands to himself and closed his eyes, both to give Adrian a little privacy and also to calm his own heart. Real privacy wasn't possible with werewolves around, but he did his best to block out the rasp of Adrian's breathing and any growls or whimpers of pain. Adrian's mood was still closely tied to his own, and if he showed how anxious he was about Adrian's shift then Adrian would get agitated himself and managing the shift would be next to impossible.

Years of self-discipline and training had given Tate the ability to slow his heartbeat at will. It was necessary if a werewolf wanted absolute control over his shift, and Tate had wanted that more than anything. Few could shift as quickly or as seamlessly as Tate, but it wasn't a point of pride for him. It was a necessity. He couldn't stand the vulnerability of the shift. For as long as it took to transform, a werewolf was helpless. Tate didn't like being helpless.

"Did it work?"

Tate's eyes shot open at the sound of Adrian's voice. Holy shit, he'd managed to shift back to his human form. That was an amazing feat—it required a huge amount of discipline for a new Turn to shift at will on their first moon.

"Goddamn, Adrian, you did it!"

Adrian's voice was husky and hoarse as he chuckled. "You seem surprised."

"I'm fucking *shocked*," Tate admitted. Adrian deserved to know how monumental what he'd accomplished was. "It's almost impossible to do that your first time. Looks like you're a natural."

Adrian's face was flushed from the pain of the shift, so Tate couldn't tell if he was blushing or not, but the sweet curve of his lips and the way he tilted his head slightly made his embarrassment clear.

"I just did what you said. The breathing thing."

"I give that speech to every wolfling I help through the Turn, and you're the first one who has ever managed to shift back before sunrise. Really, Adrian, be proud of yourself."

Adrian gave a pleased chuff and then wrinkled his nose. "Still hurt like a bitch."

"But it was faster than your first shift," Tate pointed out instead of addressing Adrian's comment about the pain. It would always hurt, but it would become less noticeable when Adrian's body learned how to work with the shift and not against it. But that wasn't something they needed to tackle tonight.

Tate felt a guilty flush creep over his own face as he realized he'd been addressing most of his comments to Adrian without looking him in the eye. Adrian was naked and sweaty, and Tate's own body was responding to his golden, glistening perfection. He needed to get Adrian dressed as soon as possible.

"You probably want a shower," he said quickly. "The bathroom is stocked with some great unscented soaps. You're going to want to take it easy on scented things now that your sense of smell is keener." He couldn't stop talking. What the hell was wrong with him? Tate never babbled. He was more of an economy of words kind of guy. No unnecessary small talk, no verbal diarrhea like what was spewing out of his mouth right now. "I'll go get the water started for you."

He bit down on his tongue to stop himself from adding anything else and scurried out of the room. He took his time fiddling with the hot and cold taps, dawdling in a way he never had before with the dozens of showers he'd started for wolflings in here before…. Those showers had been a hell of a lot less awkward than Adrian's was going to be, because since the moon hadn't set yet, Adrian had to be supervised while he took it. He'd done something amazing by controlling his shift so quickly, but that didn't mean he couldn't shift back at any moment. At least there would be a shower door between them. A flimsy, see-through door, but a door all the same.

Tate swallowed hard. Hopefully Adrian was in the mood for a scorching hot shower, one that would steam up the glass and obscure his delicious body from Tate's sight. Not that Tate needed to be able to see him—he'd seen enough of Adrian tonight to give his fantasies plenty of fodder for the next few weeks. He'd just have to be careful not to give his subconscious any more images to work with.

Tate kept his gaze averted as Adrian stumbled into the room and climbed into the shower, but the pornographic moan he let out as soon as the water hit him had Tate jamming a hand in his mouth so he didn't join in.

He turned the sink on full blast and stuck his head under the icy cold water. There were only a few hours until the moon set, and then he'd be able to get Adrian situated in a cabin far, far away.

## *Chapter Nine*

**ADRIAN** ached. Every inch of him hurt, from his toes
to his hair. He hadn't realized hair *could* hurt, but here
he was with aching hair.

All he wanted to do was curl up in a soft, warm
bed and sleep. The agony of the Turn was behind him—
fuzzy, pain-soaked memories that were already growing
hazy. He and Tate had spent the rest of the early morning
hours playing card games and taking turns reading to
each other. He'd wanted to do something different to
pass the time, but Tate had gently rebuked his awkward
attempt at a kiss, and Adrian had taken the hint.

So when he said every inch of him hurt, well, he wasn't
taking artistic license. The one part of him that hadn't been
hurt by the Turn ached from an unconsummated Turn
bond. Sleep hadn't been a possibility while he'd been

strung out on the moon and panting over Tate, but now that it had set, Adrian felt like all his strings had been cut.

He just wanted to *sleep*.

And unfortunately, until Tate finished his pissing contest with the tiny woman who'd introduced herself as Camp H.O.W.L.'s director after breakfast this morning, there wasn't anywhere for Adrian *to* sleep.

"We don't have a protocol for this," she said, her voice grating on Adrian's sensitive hearing.

"I understand that we don't have a protocol. That's why I'm suggesting he room with Harris," Tate said, voice weary. Adrian wanted to reach out and run a hand over Tate's jaw to see if the stubble that had sprouted there overnight was as prickly as it looked. Tate's hair was sandy blond, but his beard was coming in speckled with gray. Adrian wanted to lick it.

God, what was wrong with him? He wanted to *lick* Tate? Adrian groaned and pillowed his head on his arms. The table was sticky and reeked of maple syrup, but he didn't care. He hadn't been this sleep drunk since grad school. If he didn't get into a bed—any bed—soon he was going to cry.

Tate's insistence that Adrian room with someone else also made him want to cry, but he knew that was the bond talking. Tate had been nothing but kind from the moment they'd walked into the room last night. Adrian's memories of the Turn were fractured and fuzzy, but all of them were tinged with the warm feeling of safety. Tate had held up his end of the bargain, giving Adrian all the support he needed to get through the Turn and the horror of his first shift. The unconsummated bond thrummed like a sore tooth at the back of Adrian's consciousness, but he couldn't fault Tate for that. He'd been honest from the beginning that he didn't want that kind of bond with Adrian, and Adrian respected that.

Tate's expression was impassive, but that didn't fool Adrian. He could hear Tate's heartrate picking up, and his distress was making Adrian's instincts go wild. The bond wanted him to protect Tate. Adrian's nose twitched at the scent Tate was leaking all over the place—tangy and thick. It made Adrian's eyes water. He'd never actually smelled anxiety before, not with his human nose, but he somehow found himself absolutely positive about what it was. It was odd. Since waking this morning, he had a clarity of focus he'd never experienced before. Scents that had been muddled before were bright and distinct. Sounds that had bothered him during the first stages of the Turn were still present, but he could disengage from them now. Bright light still plagued him, but it was an annoyance, not an ice pick in his brain like it had been. If not for the pitch of Anne Marie's voice, Adrian might be able to fall asleep right there.

He opened his eyes when the already-fast heartbeat quickened even more, and Adrian realized he'd missed something important in the conversation.

"You can't be serious." The words were delivered flatly, but there was an edge to them that made Adrian's skin prickle.

"It's the practical solution," Anne Marie answered, her tone brooking no argument.

"Why are you forcing this?" Tate bit out, the words clipped.

"It's obvious the bond took," Anne Marie said, and Adrian lifted his head to watch the two of them face off.

Tate's jaw clenched so hard Adrian worried his teeth might crack. "We didn't consummate it."

Her nose wrinkled. "That much is obvious. Why you denied yourself that is less so, but it's not my business."

"Exactly!" Tate threw his hands up. "None of this is your business."

Anne Marie didn't say a word, but Adrian could tell Tate had crossed a line. Her expression turned glacial, and Adrian had to suppress a whine.

"He is staying with you. End of discussion." Her tone made the hair on the back of Adrian's neck stand up. She was the Alpha, and she'd just laid down the law.

But Tate didn't back down so much as a fraction of an inch, which was impressive. Adrian wanted to obey and he wasn't even in her Pack. That had to mean Tate wasn't either. If he was, he'd be bowing his head right now, not holding her gaze.

A frisson of fear ran through Adrian. Unfinished bond or not, his body was reacting like his mate was being threatened. He reached out, suddenly desperate for contact, and put a hand on Tate's arm, his thumb grazing over the soft skin of his inner elbow.

Tate blew out a harsh breath but didn't shake him off. He looked down at Adrian, his expression morphing from anger to concern. Tate sank back down onto the bench and put an arm around Adrian's shaking shoulders. Adrian leaned into him, his lips tingling as they brushed against Tate's jaw. *Did that count as a lick*? he wondered, hysterical laughter bubbling up.

"Shit. It's okay, Adrian. You're just coming down from the adrenaline of the Turn."

"Which is why he'll do best with you," Anne Marie said. "You've clearly got a strong bond. Being apart will only make things worse for him."

Adrian was not in favor of any plan that made things worse. "Please," he muttered against Tate's neck. He felt rather than heard Tate's sigh.

"Of course," Tate said, like he hadn't just been willing to go toe-to-toe with an Alpha to prevent it.

Relief crashed through Adrian. A bed. He finally had a bed, and now he could go to sleep. He struggled to his feet, unsteady but determined. Heat flashed up his spine and his skin erupted in pinpricks of pain. His senses exploded, and suddenly the sticky-sweet scent of the syrup on the table made him gag.

The room swam, and Adrian saw the table rushing up to meet him.

## Chapter Ten

**"YES,** I can see how well you did keeping the bond platonic," Anne Marie said, her tone laced with amusement.

Tate glared at her from his place on the floor, where he was cradling Adrian's head in his lap. Adrian had scared the living shit out of him when he'd started to shift and passed out. He couldn't be held responsible for things he'd said in the heat of the moment—like calling Adrian baby. He'd never live that down. Luckily Adrian hadn't heard him. Unfortunately, Anne Marie had.

"Of course you'd find this funny," Tate snapped. He took the blanket Diann had run to the infirmary to grab and draped it around Adrian's prone body. Adrian had started shivering before he'd fainted, and even though Diann had sworn he was fine after they'd called her to examine him, Tate didn't fully believe her. The logical side of him knew Adrian's shivers were a side effect of the hormone and adrenaline drop and not an actual chill, but he still felt better wrapping him up.

"I don't find the *situation* funny," Anne Marie said sharply. "It's your complete inability to accept it that is mildly amusing."

"Every part of this is serious," Diann broke in, looking at both of them with disapproval. "Anne Marie, would you mind giving us some privacy?"

Tate almost hoped Anne Marie said no. He wasn't in a hurry to hear anything Diann couldn't say in front of the director. But of course she didn't.

Diann waited until the door at the top of the stairs clicked shut before turning back to Tate.

"You can talk about rules and distance all you want, but the fact of the matter is you two share a deeper connection than a simple Turn bond can account for. For your bond to be this intense without consummation...." She trailed off and offered him a small, apologetic smile. "It's something out of a fairy tale."

*Please don't say it*, Tate begged silently. He'd felt the connection to Adrian from the moment he'd walked into Adrian's hospital room, but he'd ignored it. He didn't believe in fate. The idea that werewolves had perfect matches out there waiting for them was ludicrous.

"Turn bonds are just endorphins and neurochemicals," he said, ignoring the part of him that screamed it wasn't. "It will fade."

"So is love," Diann snapped. She took a deep breath, and when she addressed him again she was using the same voice he used for recalcitrant patients. "Not all Turn bonds fade. And not all relationships are predatory. You're thirty-two, Tate. There's a lot you haven't seen. Don't let your fear over what you *have* seen influence the rest of your life."

Tate swallowed hard. He'd grown up the youngest son of an abusive, egotistical Alpha and conditioned to believe that Weres were slaves to their instincts. More wolf than human. Cruel. Every campfire story about Weres gone bad was held up as an example of what they should be like. Even the sweet stories had been co-opted into something dark. Turn bonds that involved devotion at first sight, Weres who were fated to be together—those had been his father's bread and butter. Tate had spent his entire childhood being trained to believe they were real. That when he came of age, when he came into his wolf, he'd be gifted with moonmates of his own. Plural. Because as the son of the Alpha, that was his due, just as it was his father's and his brothers'. He'd seen his sisters married off to older, mean-spirited werewolves who their father swore were their moonmates. He'd watched two of his older brothers start families of their own with girls hardly old enough to shift.

It wasn't a life he'd ever wanted, and he'd escaped it as soon as he could. And now the carefully constructed world he'd made for himself in the decade since was coming crashing down around his ears.

Tate's stomach rolled in disgust. He was more than a bundle of neurotransmitters and hormones, but it was a fight to remind himself of that in Adrian's presence.

"I know it's hard to hear, but it's the truth," Diann said gently. "Take him back to your cabin. He's fine. He just blew through his energy reserves. This has to be an incredible strain on his body. He'll wake up starving in a few hours."

Tate didn't want Adrian in his cabin, but he also couldn't bear not to have him close. His instincts were going wild at the mere thought of being separated from Adrian, especially when Adrian was in such a vulnerable state.

"I'll come by and check in on him around lunchtime," Diann said. "He might need an IV for some hydration if he doesn't wake up and get some water in him."

Worry bit at Tate. "Should he be in the infirmary?"

Diann smirked. "Would you let him be?"

"If that's the best place for him, then yes," Tate answered, staring her down. He didn't add that he'd be staying there with Adrian if that was the case, but from the way Diann's smirk grew into a genuinely pleased smile, he didn't have to.

"If his condition changes, then it might be. But for now, he's just exhausted. He'll sleep better in your cabin than he would in the infirmary."

Tate sighed but stopped fighting the inevitable. There was no denying he and Adrian shared a particularly deep Turn bond. Adrian would recover faster surrounded by Tate's scent and away from other people who he might view as a threat. Everyone would be safer this way, and Tate would be remiss not to weigh the well-being of the campers and staffers as well as Adrian's and his own.

"I'm not—this isn't what you think it is," Tate said as he gathered Adrian in the blanket and lifted him. "That doesn't—it isn't a real thing. You know it's not." He fixed Diann with a hard look. She bowed her head slightly. She might not know all the details of his past, but he'd told her enough over the years that she should know pushing the notion of a moonmate bond was a bad idea. "Get him healthy, and we'll talk about it later," she said softly.

There was a finality to her tone that assured Tate the discussion was only being tabled, not dismissed. The only thing he'd accomplish by arguing now would be delaying getting Adrian comfortably installed in Tate's cabin. That wasn't something he was wild about doing, but there wasn't any point putting it off. Besides, Adrian's dead weight was starting to make Tate's arms ache.

"There isn't anything to talk about," he said flatly as he juggled his load so his bicep was supporting Adrian's head and started toward the stairs. "As soon as this damn Turn bond wears off, everything will go back to normal."

Diann ran ahead and hit the steps first, not bothering to look over her shoulder at him to make sure he was following as she spoke.

"It would take me an hour to unpack that statement alone," she said sweetly. She opened the door at the top of the steps and held it for him.

Tate angled Adrian so he didn't risk whacking his head or legs on the doorframe and passed through without comment.

"And speaking of unpacking—"

"Which we weren't," he muttered, lengthening his stride as he crossed through the infirmary.

"—Anne Marie has already had Adrian's things brought to your cabin. Not that he had much. We'll have to arrange to get him some toiletries and clothes."

The jealous monster that had taken up residence in Tate's chest flared to life. "He can borrow mine."

Diann tutted at him reproachfully. "The man needs his own things, Tate. He must have been staying somewhere in Indianapolis. Surely he has a suitcase of things waiting for him there. I'll have Anne Marie call his Alpha and see if we can figure out how to get his luggage sent here."

That tamed Tate's inner beast. He'd assumed she meant find things to borrow here at the camp. Tate didn't want Adrian covered in anyone's scent but his own, and even if he wasn't feeling so inexplicably possessive, he very much doubted Adrian would *want* to have someone else's scent on him.

Diann had followed him all the way to the infirmary's door, and he paused there to make eye contact with her.

"Is this as bad as I think it is?"

She offered him a small smile. "Who says it's bad?"

Diann and Anne Marie had both lost their goddamn minds. How could this be anything *but* bad? Adrian was a wolfling. He was one of their campers! Any relationship with him was inappropriate, even if Tate put aside his professional reservations, which his body seemed to have done without his consent yesterday. His mind was slowly catching up, but he couldn't tell if his panic was because of those lingering concerns or because of how quickly this simple Turn bond was morphing into something more.

"I do," he said bluntly. "I say it's bad."

Diann shook her head. "Get him home and then take a shower and get some sleep. Things will be clearer after you've rested."

Tate shouldered open the door and was halfway to his cabin before he realized he hadn't called her on her use of the word home. It had felt natural to think of his home as Adrian's too.

God. He was fucked.

## *Chapter Eleven*

**ADRIAN'S** mouth was so parched his lips were sealed shut. He licked at his mouth with his dry, swollen tongue. Waking up like this was becoming an alarming habit.

He sat up and rubbed at his eyes, blinked away the haze of sleep as he looked around. He was in a sparsely furnished room, but it wasn't the one he'd spent last night in for his Turn. What had happened? How had he ended up here, and where *was* here?

He looked down at the sheets pooled around his waist. The plain white T-shirt he was wearing bagged around the shoulders a bit and was roomy through the chest. When he dared peek under the sheet he saw he was wearing a pair of threadbare red-plaid cotton pajama bottoms that were not his.

He remembered getting dressed this morning, so something had definitely happened. He glanced around the room to confirm he was alone before he ducked his head and pulled the collar of the shirt up to take a quick, self-conscious sniff. His mouth watered at the clean, comforting scent. Pine needles and wood smoke. This was Tate's.

Adrian pushed the sheet back and climbed carefully out of bed. He felt wobbly and tired but more himself than he had in days. The fog that had plagued him seemed to have lifted, and aside from an almost pleasant ache in his muscles and joints, he felt great. Thirstier than he'd ever been in his life and starving, but great.

The room had an attached bathroom with the door ajar, so he explored that first. He turned on the faucet and ducked his head to drink directly from the tap, gulping down the sweet, cold water until his mouth felt less fuzzy and the ache in his throat had subsided.

Thirst quenched, Adrian cupped his hands under the stream and splashed his face. A pile of folded towels sat on the counter, so he helped himself to one and dried off his face and neck. He felt human again after the drink and the rinse—which made him chuckle to himself. One thing he'd never be was human. That was going to take some getting used to. Would he still be the black sheep of the family now that he could join the Pack fully?

God, his family. He needed to call his mother. She and his sister were probably freaking out by now. How long had it been since he woke up in the hospital? He wasn't sure. One day? Maybe two?

The hole in his memory nagged at him like a sore tooth. Something had happened, and since he had no memory of it, it probably wasn't anything good.

A sharp knock sounded, and he poked his head out of the bathroom in time to see Tate open the bedroom door and peek around it.

"You're up," Tate said, sounding pleased. He preened inside at the approval in Tate's voice.

Adrian couldn't stem the tide of questions that erupted. "What am I doing here? Is this your cabin? What happened? What day is it?"

Tate held his hands up in a motion of surrender. "One thing at a time. How are you feeling?"

He opened the door fully and stepped into the room, and the first thing Adrian noticed was that Tate was wearing different clothes from the last time Adrian remembered seeing him.

"I'm fine," Adrian said, waving a hand dismissively. "What happened? Why would you be worried about how I was feeling? How long have I been here?"

Tate crossed the room and opened a cabinet, revealing a miniature fridge like the one in the infirmary's basement. He took out a bottle of luridly blue liquid and twisted the cap off before handing it to Adrian, who took it reflexively.

"I'm worried about how you're feeling because you had a stressful Turn and ended up starting to shift again and passing out before you'd had a chance to build your strength back up." Tate nodded to the Gatorade in Adrian's hand. "Drink it or you'll end up with another IV."

"Another IV?" Adrian echoed, looking down at the drink. He took a tentative sip. It was overly sweet, but not too bad. He drank again.

"It's Monday. You slept for almost twenty-six hours. You were here for most if it—Diann brought you back to the infirmary to monitor you when you didn't wake up after twelve hours, but she let you come back here with an IV. It was just to keep you hydrated and get some nutrients into you."

Adrian's stomach growled as if on cue, and he rested a hand over it, embarrassed.

"That's a good sign. I'll have someone bring over some food for you while you get cleaned up. I put some clothes I think will fit you in the dresser, and Diann had a new toothbrush sent over for you. You're welcome to use any of my things in the bathroom until we can get your stuff from Indy. Your family called the hotel and explained you'd had a medical emergency. They were supposed to pack up your suitcase and ship it yesterday. It should be here soon."

As confused and disoriented as he was, Adrian still thrilled a bit at the mention of sharing Tate's toiletries. This must be his cabin, then. The sheets smelled fresh but didn't carry Tate's scent, so it had to be a guest room. He fought down a spike of disappointment. Being with Tate felt right, but not being in Tate's bed felt wrong in a way Adrian couldn't explain. His mind still felt muddled and he couldn't think straight. He needed help.

"I need to call home," Adrian said. "Did my phone make it here?"

Tate nodded toward the top of the dresser, and Adrian saw the familiar white rectangle. "You had your phone on you but no charger. Luckily Harris found one for you in the camp's lost and found. Anne Marie—the director, you met her, but I'm not sure you'll remember that—has been giving your Alpha updates, but I'm sure she'll be relieved to hear from you."

Tate backed away toward the door. "I'll leave you in peace to make your call. Now that you're up, I have to get back to my classes. Do you think you'll be okay here? Diann will be over soon to check on you, I'm sure, and Harris or someone else will bring some food from the mess hall for you. I'll be back in a few hours. There's a camp directory list in the main room of the cabin. If you need something, you can call Diann or Kenya."

Tate's easy confidence was rapidly disappearing, as was his relaxed smile. Adrian was sure he hadn't misread Tate's cheerful happiness at finding him awake, so why was he suddenly desperate to get away?

"Tate? Did something happen?" Adrian paused, trying to find the right words. "Something... bad? You seem anxious."

Tate froze in the doorway. He turned around slowly, guilt creeping over his face. "I'd prefer you talk about it with Kenya. She'll be your assigned counselor while you're here."

Adrian's heart quickened. "You said I shifted. Did I hurt someone?"

"No! No, nothing like that. You didn't even finish your shift. Your body started but stopped after you passed out."

"It's just—you seem in a hurry to leave. I thought maybe I'd hurt you. I don't remember how I got here or what I did."

Tate closed his eyes for a brief moment and then stepped back into the room and leaned against the door doorframe. "I've just had some trouble processing," Tate said. That clarified nothing, Adrian thought grimly.

"We have a Turn bond," Tate continued, "but there's something more. The connection I feel to you—it's outside the scope of the regular bond. I don't know what you're feeling, but for me, it's deeper. A normal Turn bond would mean being concerned for your health and having my senses tuned to you so I can make sure you're safe. This—it's not just that. And it didn't go away this morning, like one should. I don't know what's going on, but I promise we're looking into it."

Adrian could *taste* Tate's anxiety. That must be what he was talking about. Adrian hadn't ever experienced the Turn bond, so he had nothing to compare this to. But Tate was right; there was more there. His entire body felt like it was tuned-in to Tate's, and Tate was all he could think about. Right now he should be freaking out about being newly Turned. His biggest concern should be getting on the phone with his Alpha and shoring up that connection, getting reassurance from the leader of his Pack. That instinct was there, but it took a back seat to his concern for Tate. That wasn't normal.

"Maybe you should start at the beginning," Adrian said slowly, still trying to wrap his mind around everything that had changed in the last twenty-four hours. "I remember coming through the Turn and my first shift, and I remember shifting back and spending the rest of the night talking. What happened after breakfast?"

Tate took a long breath, like he was fortifying himself. "Nothing. Really. You were exhausted and wrung out from the Turn, and you started to shift. Your body couldn't handle it, and you passed out. Diann checked you out and said you needed hydration and rest, so she gave you some IV fluids. You woke up about an hour after she pronounced you well enough to stop them."

That explained the slight bruise and soreness in his inner elbow. He rubbed at it absently. "Did they sedate me?"

"No, you slept on your own. Diann said you'd told her you hadn't been sleeping well lately, and she said it was just exhaustion, plain and simple."

Adrian mustered his courage to ask the one question Tate had skirted around. "So why are you so eager to leave, if everything is fine?"

Tate didn't answer for a long moment, and Adrian wondered if he was trying to think of a way to sidestep the issue. "The bond," Tate said finally. "I'm not comfortable with the bond."

Adrian wilted. Why would Tate want this kind of bond with him? He'd been honest about that from the start, and obviously nothing had changed. "Right," he murmured.

Tate growled and ran a hand through his hair, leaving it sticking up in all directions. "It's not you—"

"Oh God," Adrian interrupted, holding up a hand. "For the love of the moon, don't feed me the 'it's not you, it's me' line. You don't want any kind of bond with me, and you're saddled with one. And I'm sorry about that, even though there's nothing I can do about it. But if you respect me at all, don't give me a weak-ass speech about how I'm not your type or why we're incompatible. I'm a big boy, Tate. I can handle rejection. Just don't sugarcoat it, okay? That makes it worse."

Tate swallowed visibly and looked away. "We are compatible. That's the thing. And I'm more attracted to you than I've ever been to anyone. *That's* the problem. It scares me. I don't do relationships, and then this happens. It's a lot to deal with. And I realize what a jackass I sound like right now, okay? I hate that, and it makes it worse. You're going through a huge, shocking change, and then there's this wacked-out bond thrown on top of it with a broken, angry guy who doesn't believe in that kind of mumbo jumbo. You're the one with the bad luck, and all I can do is make it about me. I'm sorry."

The words had spilled lightning fast out of Tate, and Adrian was struggling to keep up. Tate thought he was broken? Adrian's mind churned over the words. Tate hadn't once said he wasn't interested in Adrian—just that Adrian shouldn't be interested in *him.* He wasn't sure what the "mumbo jumbo" Tate mentioned was, but he could guess. Adrian had grown up with the stories about Turn bonds that lasted a lifetime, and the romantic in him had always hoped they were true. As an adult he'd dismissed lifetime bonds and other fairytales as nothing more than myth, pretty stories to encourage Weres to mate with other Weres, keeping the gene pool strong. But what if they weren't?

Adrian wasn't firing on all cylinders yet, and he could see how uncomfortable the conversation was making Tate. "I'm still really confused," he admitted, "but I don't think we're going to sort anything out like this. I need to call my family, and maybe we can talk again tonight."

Tate's shaky breath was all the confirmation Adrian needed.

"If you have something to do, I won't keep you here. Maybe I'll try to go talk to Kenya after I get everything sorted out with my mom."

Tate straightened from his slouch against the door. "She'll be able to explain everything better than

I can. I'm in session all afternoon, but I can come by her office after dinner. Maybe this would be easier on neutral ground."

That sounded pretty damn ominous, but Adrian didn't push it. If Tate didn't want to talk here, he'd honor that. This was Tate's home, after all. Adrian was just a visitor.

His chest twinged at the thought of leaving in a few weeks like he knew he'd have to. He added that to his mental list of things to ask Kenya about—this sudden and heavy attachment to Tate.

Tate rapped his knuckles against the doorframe with a nod in Adrian's direction and then retreated down the hallway. Adrian stood stock-still until he heard the cabin door swing shut and then retreated to his unmade bed to sit. Standing for the short amount of time he'd been up had taken a lot out of him.

He needed food, he realized. He'd call home to update his mom, grab a shower and get dressed, and then wander around in search of something to eat. He felt better having a plan, even if it was just a loose one. The tightness in his chest eased, and he got up to grab his phone from the dresser to make what he was sure was going to be one of the most interesting phone calls of his life.


**ADRIAN** hated psychologist's offices, but Kenya's was more inviting than any he'd been in before. Hell, Kenya herself was nothing like the half-dozen therapists who'd come before her, trying to pry into Adrian's brain to figure out why he hadn't Turned as a teenager.

It still wasn't a comfortable place to be, and Adrian had to tamp down the inclination to bolt. Seeing Kenya was part of the program here at the camp, and he'd be a fool to try to pretend he didn't need someone to talk things out with.

Which was why he was surprised when she started off talking about Tate instead of him.

"Tate has given me permission to share some of his personal history with you," Kenya said after she'd settled Adrian into a cozy chair. "Normally anything a patient says to me is in complete confidence, but this is a bit of a different case. I want you to know that unless you give me similar instructions, everything we talk about today is just between the two of us. You are under no obligation to give me permission to share what we talk about with Tate, and he knows that."

She leaned forward and put a hand on his knee, squeezing it quickly before releasing it. "And that goes for your Alpha too. I won't share anything we talk about with anyone."

She settled back in her chair and took out a notebook. "Let's talk about you. I'll be your counselor while you're here, which means you can come to me with any problems you're having. They don't have to be about the Turn—they can be about anything. How have you felt today? You've been through a lot of big changes, and you've lost some time because of your exhaustion. Are you disoriented? Frustrated?"

He was plenty frustrated, but it didn't have anything to do with his Turn. "I'm wrapping my head around it," he said, the automatic response he'd given to everyone he'd talked to today. There had been a parade of phone calls; the one to his mother had just been the tip of the iceberg.

"Adrian," Kenya said, her tone stern. "It's a lot to absorb, yes. But you are a grown man who's suddenly thrust into a second puberty. Your life has been disrupted by the Turn twice now, once when it failed to happen and again when it did happen. You are allowed to be conflicted." She folded her hands in her lap and looked at him expectantly.

"I'm not conflicted about finally Turning. This is—" His voice broke, and he took a moment to compose himself. "It's all I've ever wanted. And I accepted it wasn't going to happen and made my peace with being human."

"But then the rug got ripped out from under you."

He nodded. "And I'm thrilled. Like, I don't even have words. I still can't believe this is happening. But it's complicated. And this thing with Tate—that's complicated too, especially because I'm not sure what's going on."

"And how does your Alpha feel about everything?"

Adrian's talk with his mother had gone well earlier. She was, to borrow a human phrase, over the moon at his Turning. He was sure she'd already started planning an epic coming-home party for him. He'd mentioned the Turn bond as part of his assurances that his Turn had gone smoothly, since she'd been worried. But something had stopped him from naming Tate when he'd talked about it, and he also hadn't gone into how he and Tate shared an abnormally strong Turn bond.

He'd told himself he didn't want to cause her any undue anxiety, but really he just didn't want to share any part of Tate yet—and that included his existence. It felt too new and too huge, paired with how uncertain everything was at the moment, to talk about with her. She'd want to know what would happen next, and the truth was he didn't know.

Maybe Kenya did.

"I haven't told her about Tate. Is he coming?" Adrian asked, looking around for a clock. There were none. Kenya's office was done in soft tones with light, overstuffed furniture, and not a clock to be seen.

"Tate is planning to join us in a bit" she said. "He didn't want to be here for this part. Understandably. It's important for you to know Tate's history, but he doesn't like talking about it. Tate's childhood…." She appeared to be searching for how to continue, and Adrian held his breath, waiting for her to finish. "It wasn't like yours, or mine, or anyone's really."

Adrian's childhood had been wonderful. Two loving parents, child of the Alpha, homeschooled by his father, who was a teacher, until high school, then sent to an expensive private school. Siblings and cousins to play with. A house that was always full of laughter.

"He grew up in Idaho," she said, making eye contact with Adrian like that should be significant. He racked his brain, but it wasn't. He shook his head.

"Tate cut himself off from his family after he Turned. It took him a few moons to gather up the resources to leave, but he's been on his own ever since. I met him a few months after he left Idaho. He was a student in one of my psychology courses at Indiana University." She smiled when Adrian looked up.

"It's…." She shook her head and started over. "What I'm about to tell you, it's disturbing. But I don't want you to let it color how you think of Tate, as hard as that will be. He's his own man, and he's worked very hard to get where he is." She smiled fondly. "Dr. Lewis is light-years away from the scared boy I met back then. At nineteen, he was Tatum Bodkin, a kid who couldn't stop looking over his shoulder, waiting for his past to catch up to him."

Something about the name Bodkin sounded familiar, but it hovered at the edge of Adrian's memory. He recognized it as significant, but he couldn't remember why.

Kenya nodded knowingly. "Heard of his family, I assume?"

"I think I know the name, but I can't quite place it."

"His father is the Alpha of—"

That was all Adrian needed to put the pieces together. "Shit," he said, breathless. "Tate is a part of that werewolf liberation group?"

Calling it a group was kind. It was more of a cult, or at least that's how the Werewolf Tribunal viewed it.

"He's not, no," Kenya said, enunciating the words carefully. "His family is. That's why he's taken such pains to cut himself off from them, Adrian. He escaped the sect soon after his Turn and started a new life. He even changed his name when he was twenty-one. I helped him do it. He didn't want any ties to his family, and legally, he doesn't have any now."

Alpha Bodkin and his Pack were infamous among werewolves. They lived on a sprawling compound in rural Idaho, and not much was known about them other than that they believed werewolves shouldn't have to hide who they were. Aside from their remote location, they took absolutely no measures to conceal their existence. They shifted and ran as wolves whenever they wanted, and from what Adrian had heard, that was a lot of the time. They lived off the land and were completely off the grid. They were the werewolf version of the bogeyman. "If you don't behave, we'll send you to live in Idaho." Adrian had heard his sister say that to his eight-year-old nephew last week.

"He seems so normal," Adrian blurted out, shame creeping over him as soon as the words left his mouth. He sounded like a serial killer's neighbor being interviewed on a cut-rate cop drama.

"He *is* normal," Kenya snapped. She blinked and shook her head. "I'm sorry, Adrian. That wasn't very professional of me. I'm protective of him."

"I'm glad. It sounds like you were there for him when he needed someone in his corner."

She smiled. "I was. And I'm hoping you will be that person now. The two of you share something more than a regular Turn bond. I think Tate knows that, and it scares him. His father is a disturbed man, Adrian. He took so much that is wonderful about werewolf culture and perverted it. Tate still struggles to overcome some of the things he learned as a child. It's a difficult thing to do. It takes a strong person to challenge the ideology of their upbringing, but sometimes even the strongest wills falter."

Pride warmed Adrian's chest. He knew Tate was something special, but he'd had no idea how special he was. "What about his upbringing makes this situation hard for him?"

Kenya leaned forward and shook her head. "Don't you think that's a conversation you should be having with Tate?"

Adrian sighed. Logically that made the most sense. He ought to be hearing this straight out of Tate's mouth. But Tate had been so uncomfortable when they'd talked earlier, and his wolf whined at the thought of causing Tate more grief.

"You said our Turn bond was out of the ordinary, and Tate said something similar. What caused that? My fucked-up biological clock? Did he bond differently with me because I'm so old?"

"Twenty-eight. Practically ancient."

He didn't want to smile, but he couldn't help it. Something about Kenya put him at ease. "You know what I meant."

"There's no way to know why your body waited until now to Turn, but I very much doubt that this Turn bond has anything to do with your age. Our bodies are primed to form bonds with compatible people. Biologically, it ensures the survival of our species—"

"Whoa, wait," he said, throwing up a hand in alarm. "There is no 'survival of our species' in play here. I'm a dude. Tate is a dude. I know my Turn was abnormal, but it didn't give me a uterus."

A low chuckle from the doorway made Adrian jump. He whirled around and saw Tate standing there, a bemused expression on his face.

"Don't let me interrupt," he said, crossing his arms and leaning on the doorjamb. "By all means, please continue this discussion of Adrian's magical werewolf uterus."

Kenya pursed her lips. "You two deserve each other."

That wiped the smile off Tate's face. He stood up and stepped into the room, closing the door behind himself. "I wouldn't say that," he muttered.

"I was telling Adrian about our biological drive to find safety," she said, quirking an eyebrow at Adrian in challenge when he opened his mouth again. "And how it also helps us find compatible mates because it can cause us to bond with someone who is our perfect complement."

Well, that was a relief. "So no ass babies?"

Kenya didn't hold back her laugh at Adrian's question this time, though Tate looked completely stricken.

"Ass babies?" he asked, his voice strangled. "Jesus, Kenya!"

"Is that really so hard to believe, though?" she prodded after she'd caught her breath. "Not male werewolf pregnancy, obviously. But your bond. That two people could be the perfect complement to each other? Suited in temperament and demeanor? Physically attracted to each other from the start?"

Adrian looked between the two of them before answering. The room felt charged and tense. "Well, no."

"It's not that uncommon, you know. A Turn bond that grows into something more over time. Quite a few marriages start with a temporary bond as teenagers."

Tate scoffed. "But you're talking years with those, Ken. Adrian and I shouldn't still be bonded. The Turn bond should have broken by now."

It hadn't. Adrian could feel Tate like a presence at the back of his mind, faint but definitely there. Adrian's senses made it clear Tate was agitated—he smelled bitter and his heart was going crazy. But there was more. Tate was terrified. Adrian could practically taste the sour tang of his fear. But somewhere buried in there, lost to the chemosignals but present in Adrian's mind, was a niggle of something else. Tate was angry and scared, but somewhere deep down he was also excited and—hopeful?

"What are you scared of?" he blurted, regretting it the moment Tate's eyes went wide and his scent soured even more. "You're—there's nothing to be afraid of. I'm not going to force you into a bond you don't want,

Tate. I know you don't know me at all, but I'd hope you'd realize I'm not a monster."

"No one is forcing anyone into anything," Kenya said firmly. "And Adrian, Tate knows that. He's not afraid of you. You need to explain now, Tate. It's not my place, but you're causing him unnecessary upset over this."

That sounded incredibly ominous. Especially the way it made Tate's face cloud.

"We don't—"

"We do," Tate said grimly. "We've been calling our connection a Turn bond, but Kenya and Diann think it's more than that."

He looked absolutely sick, and Adrian wanted to rush forward and make him stop talking. He had to force himself to stay in his chair. Kenya pointed Tate toward the couch, but Tate shook his head. They locked gazes for a long moment before Kenya sighed.

"What do you know about moonmates, Adrian?"

That wasn't what he'd been expecting at all. He'd heard of moonmates—everyone knew the fairytale of the two wolflings from warring Packs who were bonded at first sight. The stories said they were fated to be together and blessed by the moon herself.

Their history was dotted with stories of other moonmated couples who came after the first pair. There were no modern stories about moonmates, and the easiest explanation for that was that they didn't exist. Occam's razor. The simplest explanation was usually the right one.

"I know the stories," he said, keeping a careful watch on Tate's impassive face. "But that's all they are. Stories."

"I believe in them," Kenya said solemnly. "Oh, most of those stories are probably made up. But I've seen it happen. And I'm seeing it happen again here. You could argue that they are just well-matched couples who fell in love, and that would be true. That there wasn't a destiny component to it—and maybe there wasn't. Maybe it's just an antiquated term to describe a couple who are perfect for each other and who fall in love quickly. But that doesn't explain the connection between them—how quickly they are able to get inside each other's heads and truly *know* that person."

She shook her head ruefully. "It sounds so juvenile, I know. But how else do you explain the way you feel about Tate? You're sensitive to his moods—preternaturally so. He's half in love with you already, and that's extremely out of character for him. Tate closes himself off and doesn't let anyone in. But you're already through the door. I can't explain it."

Tate coughed but didn't correct her. His cheeks were flaming.

Adrian didn't have a logical way to explain away the feelings he'd developed, literally overnight. He wasn't the type to fall into a crush this hard, yet here he was. The fact that Tate seemed to be in the same boat gave him a perverse satisfaction that both excited him and turned his stomach. But moonmates? That was hard to swallow. He glanced over at Tate, who seemed to be trying to memorize the pattern in the tile.

"Is that why you're so angry?" he asked Tate, his throat tight. "You think you're stuck being moonmated to me?"

Tate's head shot up. "I told you, it doesn't have anything to do with *you*. I just—it's not you, okay? It's the situation."

"The situation is you freaking out because you're bonded to me," Adrian said sharply. "And I'm getting tired of the mixed signals. Because to hear Kenya talk, you feel the same way I do. But it's obvious you don't want this, so I have no idea what to do with any of this."

"You don't have to 'do' anything," Tate said. "This isn't your issue. It's mine, and I don't plan on letting it interfere with your experience here at Camp H.O.W.L."

So Tate had finally found his tongue. Too bad he wasn't using it to say anything Adrian wanted to hear. Anger spiked through him. "That's a bullshit line and you know it," Adrian seethed. "If we really do share this rare bond, do you honestly think walking away from it is going to be easy at the end of the month?"

Tate's jaw clenched, and Adrian reveled in the flash of anger he felt through the bond. Good. Let Tate get riled up. He wanted to see some sort of emotion from him to reassure himself that Tate was in this just as much as he was.

"The thought of you walking away from me makes me want to throw something," Tate said, and Adrian was shocked into silence by his unexpected honesty. "Is that what you want me to say? That I want you? I do. That I feel this sense of *wrongness* when we're not together? That's true too. But we're not wolves, we're people. We aren't slaves to our instincts."

Heat flared over Adrian's skin at Tate's words. Suddenly there didn't seem to be enough air in the room.

"Take a moment," Kenya said, her words measured and calm.

Adrian wanted more than a moment. His palms itched and his skin felt too small. He couldn't seem to draw enough air in no matter how hard he tried. He was losing control.

"Adrian, this is perfectly normal." Kenya's voice sounded like it was under water. Hazy and indistinct, more like the memory of someone talking than someone sitting a foot away from him. "You've been through a lot, physically and emotionally. Your control will come with time. Just let it happen."

Shivers of heat speared up his spine, like knives sliding through flesh and ripping it apart. His tensed muscles cramped and spasmed, and he heard the arm of the chair he was sitting in snap as he gripped it.

"Don't fight your shift. You'll only make it more painful," Kenya said.

That sounded like great advice, but it wasn't helpful in the least. Adrian had no idea what to do. He wasn't fighting anything—it was like the shift was attacking him. Agony washed over him in waves, building and receding with increasing frequency. If he knew how to stop this he would.

Sweat stung his eyes and he blinked furiously, trying to clear it away so he could see. His back bent under the next roll of the shift, and he slid off the couch and onto the floor. The cool tile pressed against his cheek helped ground him, and he focused on that instead of the pain.

He focused on drawing in slow, steady breaths. It held the worst of the pain at bay, but he couldn't push the shift all the way back. He hadn't fully shifted, but his fingers were tipped with claws and coarse hair had sprouted up his arms. He was caught in some sort of torturous limbo.

Adrian turned his head and watched as Tate lay down next to him.

"Are you going for a record?" Tate's expression was strained, and Adrian could feel the concern coming off him, but his tone was teasing. "Most shifts in twenty-four hours, maybe?"

Adrian tried to smile at the lame joke, but it came out as a grimace. Having Tate close had taken the edge off his anxiety and pain, but he was still suspended midshift. It wasn't a comfortable feeling.

"Practice makes perfect," Adrian managed to force out through his clenched teeth.

Tate offered him a forced smile. "You did strike me as the perfectionist type," he said. "Okay, as you've found, there's a point of no return with a shift. Early on you can back it up, but once you're reached the tipping point, the only way through is forward. It's like that famous quote. The only way through hell is to keep going."

Adrian's pelvis felt like it was cracking. "Churchill," he gasped out.

"Sure," Tate said easily. "So I need you to stop fighting the shift. Let it happen."

Adrian wanted to protest that he *wasn't* fighting, but he couldn't open his mouth. His jaw felt like it weighed a hundred pounds. The pressure in his skull was unbearable.

"Remember how you guided your shift back to human? You envisioned how things feel different in your human body, and that triggered your shift. You can do the same thing to help this along. How did the air taste as a wolf? It was amazing, wasn't it? Think of everything your human nose isn't picking up here."

Tate took a deep breath, and Adrian watched him through hooded eyes, his attention locked on Tate's face.

"Woodsmoke. With your wolf nose, you'll be able to pinpoint exactly which cabin it's at," he continued. "Some of the leaves out in the forest are already starting to drop, and you'll be able to tell what kind and where they are. Leaves that have fallen have a different scent—a layer of decay. Right now the entire forest smells like the change of seasons. And in the spring? In the spring you'll be able to smell all that new life as buds start to sprout leaves. There's nothing like it. It smells *vibrant*."

Adrian closed his eyes and listened to Tate's voice. He'd mostly smelled the stink of his own fear when he'd Turned, but there had been a lot of nuances to the air that it hadn't blocked out entirely, like the piney-sharp scent of whatever they'd cleaned the room with contrasting with the real pine scent carried in with the air from outside.

He licked his lips, seeking out the tastes carried on the air. Tate was right—with a wolf's nose, scent was more than just a smell. It was an experience. It didn't register on his tongue, but rather at the back of his throat. He could pick up the mildewed scent of decay Tate had mentioned, mild but definitely there. Kenya's scent was layered into the room, probably from years of using it. The chair in the corner by the window was her favorite—he could tell because it was where her scent was concentrated. A bit stale, but heavier there than anywhere else. She hadn't been in the chair today.

He blinked open his eyes and looked around. Kenya wasn't in the room at all anymore. Adrian flexed his legs, surprised when he couldn't straighten them. He looked down and jolted when he realized he'd shifted completely. His borrowed sweatpants were shredded, and the shirt had probably met the same fate.

"Feeling better?" Tate sounded a bit winded himself, as if he'd been the one to have his body shattered and reformed into something new.

Adrian couldn't speak, but he nudged his muzzle up and caught Tate under the chin. Tate laughed.

"Why don't we head back to the cabin? You can hang out in this form or shift back if you want when we get there." He stood and smirked down at Adrian, who was still sprawled out on the floor. "Or you could shift here and walk back naked. Your choice."

Being self-conscious about nudity was a human construct, not a werewolf one, but Adrian still didn't relish the thought of giving the entire camp an eyeful of his junk. He got to his feet slowly, testing out his paws. He hadn't moved around much as a wolf the night of his Turn, and he was chagrined to realize he had to change the way he thought about walking. His legs slid out from under him when he tried to take a step on the slick floor, and he was sure he'd be blushing if it was possible. As it was, his high-pitched yelp had him wanting to burrow under the couch in embarrassment.

"It takes some getting used to," Tate said. "Here, I'll help."

Adrian watched with growing curiosity as Tate slipped his T-shirt over his head and unfastened his jeans. He looked away to give him some privacy when he realized Tate was undressing completely. By the time he looked back, a gorgeous tawny wolf was standing over a pile of neatly folded clothes. Adrian couldn't stop staring, but Tate didn't seem to mind. He stood still, letting Adrian circle him. Tate was thinner than Adrian would have expected, but he looked strong. His fur had the same sun-drenched highlights that Tate's hair had, which absolutely delighted Adrian. Tate gave a sharp yip to get Adrian's attention after a few more moments, long before Adrian had managed to drink in his fill of the sight of Tate fully shifted.

They couldn't communicate with words, but it didn't hinder Tate's ability to teach Adrian how to move in this body. After one more false start, his confidence grew, and Adrian was able to cross the room almost as gracefully as Tate.

The closed door didn't slow Tate down at all. It had a lever for a handle, something Adrian hadn't noticed before, but that struck him as a clever necessity now. Tate was able to open it with his muzzle, and the two of them stepped onto the gravel trail outside Kenya's office. The small, sharp rocks would have stung his human feet, but the pads of Adrian's paws were toughened, and walking on the rocks didn't cause the slightest twinge of discomfort.

Tate took the same kind of long-legged strides in his wolf form as he did as a human, and Adrian had to hurry to keep pace with him. He'd walked this route not half an hour ago as a human, but it was completely different as a wolf. Adrian kept getting distracted by scents and sounds, sometimes coming to a full stop to identify something that caught his attention.

Tate was waiting on the cabin's porch when Adrian finally caught up, his eyes alight with amusement and head tilted slightly as he watched Adrian. Adrian found it completely endearing.

Whether or not moonmates were an actual thing, there was no denying Adrian had a connection with Tate. One that was growing deeper every hour they spent together—and one he couldn't help but want to nurture, even though there was no way it could end well, not with Tate as vehemently opposed to the idea as he was.

He watched Tate nose open the cabin door and then trotted inside behind him. Besotted, Adrian thought. That was the word. Against his better judgment, he was absolutely besotted with this man.

# *Chapter Twelve*

**ADRIAN** seemed happy in his wolf form, so Tate didn't pressure him into shifting back once they'd gotten back to the cabin. He, however, wanted a beer, and since he needed thumbs to make that work, he'd have to shift back.

Watching was good practice for Adrian, so he barked sharply to grab his attention before he melted into his shift. Adrian followed hot on his heels when Tate padded down the hall, but he stopped short of following Tate into his room. As a human, a person's room was a boundary that most wouldn't invade without permission. As a wolf, it was a den, and the impulse to preserve its privacy was much stronger.

Tate could feel Adrian's growing anxiety through their bond, so he hurried through getting dressed so he could rejoin him. Adrian was standing at full alert outside the door when Tate emerged, and he ran a hand over the soft fur on top of Adrian's head as he walked by, marking Adrian with his scent to comfort him. The tension bled out of Adrian's stance as he trotted down the hall after Tate, which only intensified Tate's desire for a beer.

Adrian didn't seem that sold on the concept of moonmates, which was good. He also didn't seem against the idea of them furthering their bond, which was bad. It had disaster written all over it, but the more time Tate spent with Adrian the less that argument deterred him. Even if it was going to end with him getting his heart broken, it was too hard to fight. Tate had never wanted anyone as much as he wanted Adrian, and his resolve was wearing down.

Tate popped the top off a beer, laughing when Adrian buried his head in his paws when offered one. Tate didn't blame him. They didn't lose themselves when they shifted, not after their first time, but things were simpler as a wolf. If Adrian needed time to think, staying shifted would help. Tate, on the other hand, needed time *not* to think, hence the beer.

"You can stay shifted as long as you like," he told Adrian. "If you need me to talk you through shifting back, let me know."

He picked up a book he'd left on the coffee table and curled up on the couch. He'd barely gotten through a chapter before Adrian's hackles rose and a sharp knock sounded at the door. Tate ran a calming hand over his neck on his way to the door. From the smell of it, someone had sent over dinner.

"Kenya said you'd probably be holed up over here," Diann said as soon as he opened the door. She held a picnic basket in both hands. "Didn't want you two to go hungry."

Tate had gotten takeout from the mess hall dozens of times, and it had never come in a wicker basket before. He raised an eyebrow at her as he took it. It was heavier than he'd expected, and glassware clinked inside it.

"I thought it was taco bar night."

"I didn't want to bother the kitchen in the middle of the dinner rush," she said, her eyes sparkling with amusement when he shook his head.

"Of course you didn't."

"Enjoy." She gave him a finger wave before retreating from his porch, probably to meet up with Kenya to gossip about her meddling.

He sighed and closed the door. Adrian was on the rug, his ears perked toward the entryway, and his gaze locked on Tate.

"Diann brought us dinner," he said as he put the basket on the coffee table. "If you're hungry you can shift back now, or if not I can make a plate of stuff for you to have later."

He started unpacking the basket, his stomach rumbling as the scent of fresh bread filled the room. She'd been to the farmer's market recently. There were an assortment of cheeses and a jar of the blueberry rhubarb preserves made by a farm in Bloomington that he loved. As he'd suspected, there was also a bottle of wine and some glasses.

Tate caught the scent of Adrian's pain and turned just in time to see him shift. His brow was sweaty and his smile was more of a grimace, but he looked proud.

Adrian gave himself a once-over and pumped his fist. "Nailed it."

He tried to take a step, wobbled, and caught himself on the arm of the couch.

"Seven out of ten. Too bad you didn't stick the landing."

Adrian barked out a laugh. "I'll keep that in mind for next time."

"Go get dressed and I'll get dinner situated," Tate said. "We can eat in here and watch Netflix or something if you want."

Adrian cringed. "Would you mind if we didn't?"

Tate kept forgetting Adrian was a new Turn. He handled himself so well it was easy to treat him like one of the other counselors instead of a wolfing who was still adjusting to amped-up senses.

"Of course."

Adrian shivered as he made his way down the hall, so Tate lit a fire in the grate. Late summer was usually still sweltering during the day, but it got surprisingly cool in the evenings, tucked in the middle of the forest. By the time Adrian returned, looking cozy in a pair of Tate's pajama pants and a worn T-shirt, the fire was crackling and Tate had laid the picnic out on the rug.

Adrian hesitated before entering the room. "This is—"

"More mixed messages," Tate said. He shrugged. "I know. I keep telling you, it really isn't you. I'm the problem. I'm attracted to you, Adrian. I was before the bond, and I am now. I feel an overwhelming urge to take care of you, and I'd be lying if I said I didn't want you. But I don't like the idea that our biology is calling the shots here. I don't like having my choice taken away from me."

Adrian sank onto the rug and took the glass of wine Tate held out for him. "I get that, but you just said you were attracted to me before too. What if the bond isn't purely biological? What if it just amplifies what you're already feeling?"

Logically, it made sense. But logic didn't play a big role in the part of Tate's brain where all his insecurities lived. But Kenya and Diann were right about one thing—Tate had to stop letting his past define his future. He'd been hiding himself away for too long.

"That's probably true," he admitted. He took a sip of the wine Diann had given them and made a face. "This is sweet."

Adrian picked up the bottle. "It's a mead. They make it with honey. I think it tastes good."

Tate put his glass down and picked his beer up. Even warm, it was better than the mead. "So you like sweet wines. What else do you like?"

Despite their dramatic meeting and the bond they shared, Tate didn't know a lot about Adrian aside from what a quick Google search was able to turn up on the drive back from Indianapolis while Adrian had slept in the van.

It bothered Tate that he didn't know Adrian's favorite color or how—not if; he'd seen the guy naked—he liked to work out . If he liked cream in his coffee, or if he even liked coffee at all.

"I like all wines, not just the sweet ones," Adrian said. He picked up the plate Tate had made for him and popped a piece of cheese into his mouth. "And beer, but just the darker stuff. I don't like hops."

Tate's fridge was full of hoppy beers. He had an insane urge to run out to the store to stock up on things Adrian would like. That had to be the bond, didn't it? This overwhelming need to take care of Adrian and make him happy?

"I'm not a big drinker anyway," Adrian said with a shrug. "Not a picky eater, either."

"I usually just eat what's in the mess hall, but I can grab some groceries if you'd like to cook here." He'd probably used the kitchen in the cabin a total of five times since he'd moved in, but he liked the cozy intimacy of sharing a meal alone with Adrian.

Adrian laughed. "Part of the reason I'm not a picky eater is because I don't cook. We have a big Pack— someone's always willing to have me over for dinner so I don't get scurvy from subsisting solely on cereal eaten over the sink."

From his research, Tate knew Adrian was one of four kids of one of the most prominent Alphas in the country, who in addition to running her Pack and having a seat on the Werewolf Council, also ran a business Adrian was very active in.

On the surface, Adrian was Tate's polar opposite. He'd had a wonderful childhood, at least from what Tate had read online about Adrian's family. Tate knew better than most that not everything online was true, but he really wanted it to be in this case. He had feelings for Adrian—ridiculous, maybe-bond-induced, mushy feelings—and he wanted to believe Adrian's life up until this point had been good. Not like his.

"I never learned how to cook," he said, and then gulped the rest of his beer. He never talked about his childhood, but this was different. Adrian was different. "My father believed that cooking was women's work."

Adrian shook his head. "A statement like that would cause a riot in my Pack."

That was part of Tate's hesitancy to get involved with Adrian. He and Adrian came from very different backgrounds, and as the son of the Alpha, Adrian held an important place in his Pack.

"There were a lot of things I had to unlearn when I left," Tate said. "Some of it I knew was wrong, but things like that seemed natural until I got out."

"I bet those were some tough lessons to learn," Adrian said, and Tate was floored to hear sympathy in his voice instead of judgment.

"Kenya had to teach me how to do my laundry," he admitted. "Among other things. I was pretty pathetic."

Adrian leaned over and caught his eye. "You're not pathetic. You're amazing. You had to be so brave to leave. I can't imagine."

Adrian wasn't the first person to tell him that, but he was the first person Tate believed. How could he not, when he could feel Adrian's pride and admiration bursting through their bond? He closed the distance between them and kissed him. Adrian tasted like the sweet honeyed mead he'd been drinking, and Tate deepened the kiss, sweeping his tongue into Adrian's mouth, seeking more. He didn't mind it at all when it was tempered with Adrian's own intoxicating taste.

He gave himself over to the simple pleasure of the kiss for several long moments before reluctantly pulling back. There were things Adrian needed to know about him before they took this much further. Things he wasn't ready to tell him right now.

Adrian rested his head against Tate's neck as they caught their breath. "Not that I'm complaining, but you were pretty adamant that we not consummate the bond. I need to know if you've changed your mind."

Tate tucked his cheek against the top of Adrian's head. "I want to take things slow, but yeah. There's just something irresistible about you."

**TATE** took a breath and balanced the tray he'd brought over from the mess hall so he could rap his knuckles against Adrian's bedroom door. Breakfast had ended twenty minutes ago, and Tate didn't want Adrian to miss out because he'd slept through it. They'd stayed up late talking after their impromptu picnic, and Tate hadn't had the heart to wake Adrian when he'd left this morning. Adrian had said he wasn't picky about food, so Tate brought a bit of everything. He had tea, coffee, eggs, bacon, a cinnamon roll, fruit, and a yogurt— surely something on the tray would make Adrian happy.

He heard the bed creak, and a moment later Adrian opened the door, his face flushed and creased from sleep and his dark hair sticking up in all directions. He looked adorable, and Tate bit down hard on his tongue to stop himself from saying it out loud.

Adrian blinked owlishly at him. "Tate?"

Tate realized he'd been standing there staring dumbly. He thrust the tray toward Adrian, whose gaze traveled down to it in confusion.

"Breakfast," Tate explained. Adrian backed up from the door to give him space, and Tate stepped inside and put the tray on the dresser. "You can't skip meals right now—your metabolism is all over the place because of the Turn, and every time you shift you burn an insane amount of calories."

Adrian yawned. "What time is it?"

"Just after ten." Tate started to step back out of the room to give him some privacy, but Adrian stopped him.

"Is this normal? Being so tired?"

That must mean Adrian didn't usually sleep this much. Tate tucked that nugget of information away in his growing mental file. "Can be. It's a lot for your body to adjust to."

Most of the campers slept late as a rule, so Tate didn't know if this was unusual or not. Breakfast was sparsely attended on days classes didn't start early, and even on days the wolflings had to be up anyway, they usually swept through to grab coffee and something they could eat on the go.

Not coincidentally, breakfast was Tate's favorite meal of the day. He'd always been an early riser, but a meal without noise and crowds was all the incentive he needed to rise at dawn most days. He'd already eaten, gotten in a run, and attended Blake's morning yoga class before grabbing Adrian's food.

Adrian rubbed a hand over his face and studied the tray. His moan when he saw the coffee was almost pornographic. "Magic elixir of life," he muttered, taking the mug in both hands and breathing in the steam.

"I didn't know what you'd like, so I got a variety."

Adrian's grateful smile made Tate weak in the knees. Literally. He had to lean against the doorframe to stay upright. He'd never had a reaction to someone like that before. Hell, he'd never even known a reaction like that was physically *possible*.

"I appreciate it." Adrian dipped a spoon in the yogurt. "I'm not usually a big breakfast person, but I'm starving."

"That's normal too," Tate offered. He looked past Adrian and out the window, not wanting the image of him licking the spoon in his mental catalog. He was already thrumming with arousal at the sight of Adrian all rumpled—after last night's kiss he didn't need any more fodder for his overactive libido. Adrian seemed to be well ahead of the other wolflings in terms of interpreting chemosignals, so Tate doubted his interest had gone unnoticed. Luckily Adrian was kind enough not to mention it—just like Tate was adult enough not to focus on the fact that he could smell how he was affecting Adrian too. "It'll take a few months, but your appetite will return to normal. You'll only need to eat more when you're shifting a lot."

Adrian swallowed his bite, and Tate chanced a glance at him. He was eating some bacon now, which seemed a lot safer than the spoon for Tate's peace of mind.

"Everyone keeps telling me how much things are going to settle in the next few months," Adrian said, his lip curled slightly. "But how? Is it just a biological thing? Is it a control thing? What can I do to hurry it along?"

"Control will help, but some of it is just timing. We think of the Turn happening over a day or so, but really it takes a good month for all those hormones to settle down. You're able to shift now, and your body has gone through most of the changes from the Turn, but there are still small things happening. Body chemistry, building more muscle, your bones strengthening. Things like that take a lot of energy, which is why you're tired. They also take a lot of calories, which is why you're hungry. Mood swings are common, trouble sleeping, aches and pains—it's like a hellacious growth spurt."

Adrian leaned a hip against the dresser, cradling his coffee like a precious gift. "But there are things I can do to get control faster, right?"

"Absolutely. It's why you're here. We have classes six days a week aimed at helping wolflings understand the physiological changes the Turn brings and how to maintain control. How to blend in the human world.

How to shift without so much trauma. How to take care of your body now that you're stronger."

Adrian brightened. "When do I start classes?"

"As soon as you're feeling up to it," Tate said.

Adrian put his mug on the tray and opened the dresser, pulling out a fresh pair of Tate's sweats. They were still waiting for Adrian's things, and Tate wasn't sure if he wanted them to arrive quickly or not. Having Adrian blanketed in his scent was a special kind of torture, but it was also comforting knowing part of him was with Adrian throughout the day.

"I can be ready in five."

Tate glanced at his watch. "The morning session has already started, but you can join in the afternoon sessions today if you like. Go ahead and finish your breakfast. You have plenty of time."

Adrian looked almost comically conflicted, like he wanted to eat but didn't want to miss anything.

"You can't afford to skip meals right now," Tate reminded him. A spike of satisfaction went through him when Adrian picked his fork back up and shoveled in a mouthful of eggs.

"I have a session starting in twenty minutes, so I have to go. Are you okay here? I can come by and take you over to the mess hall for lunch at twelve-thirty. You can come to my two o'clock class on social media if you want."

Adrian choked on the piece of croissant he'd just broken off and popped into his mouth. "Social media?" he asked incredulously.

Tate shrugged. "It's a huge exposure risk," he said. "Remember, these wolflings are teenagers. Their first instinct is to put everything on Instagram. Their little brains aren't fully formed yet—they don't think things through. We have to hammer in the importance of secrecy and what that means for their day-to-day lives while we have them here as a captive audience."

Adrian chuckled. "I don't have an Instagram."

"Twitter, then," Tate teased. "It's where all the old fogies are these days."

He didn't have a Twitter himself. He didn't have any social media, which at a glance made him an odd choice for teaching sessions on staying safe in the cyber world. But the reason he didn't have any of those accounts was because he knew exactly how hazardous they could be—especially for someone who was running from a dangerous, messy past like his. That never made it into his lessons, but it was the driving force behind every lecture he gave in the class. Adrian was watching him with thinly veiled amusement. "I just can't picture you teaching teenagers about social media."

"I'm not teaching them about social media. I'm teaching them how to manage their social media presence to prevent the downfall of werewolf civilization."

Adrian took a drink of coffee and quirked an eyebrow. "The downfall of civilization?"

It sounded stupid, but it was absolutely imperative that they made sure the wolflings understood how one simple Snap could start an avalanche that would be next to impossible to dig out of. Once the genie—or werewolf in this case—was out of the bottle, there was no going back. So they had to prevent the secret from getting out in the first place.

"I swear, it's going to be caused by social media," Tate insisted. "Either by a werewolf posting something stupid or a passerby seeing something that doesn't add up and taking a photo or a video that ends up going viral."

There had already been a few catastrophes, but the Werewolf Tribunal had a werewolf-run PR firm dedicated to debunking things people posted on the internet.

"I'm definitely coming to your afternoon class," Adrian said.

"I thought you didn't use social media?"

Adrian's eyes sparkled as he smiled, and Tate's heart fluttered. Honest to God *fluttered*. "I'm intrigued by the idea of seeing you up in front of a class, being all authoritative while you say things like tweet and hashtag."

Tate shook his head. "I changed my mind. Don't come to my class."

This felt like flirting—not that Tate had a lot of experience with it. It felt playful and fun, natural in a way that chatting up attractive men never had before. He was having a good time standing in the extra bedroom of his cabin shooting the shit with a newly Turned werewolf who looked like sex on a stick and had a laugh like sunshine shot through with whiskey. He was so screwed.

"You won't be able to keep me away," Adrian teased. "I'll be there in the front row. Teacher's pet."

Heat shot through Tate at the joke, and he ducked his head to hide his warming cheeks. "I'll come by to pick you up for lunch, unless you want to get out and explore on your own."

He looked up and saw Adrian's slow, pleased smile. Adrian seemed to know exactly how much Tate was enjoying their conversation. Tate could feel the happiness coming off Adrian, which led into some sort of bizarre feedback loop—he was happy because Adrian was happy, and Adrian's happiness amplified his own. Now that he'd stopped resisting it, there was no denying their connection was more than a Turn bond—even if he was uncomfortable calling it the M word.

"I'm going to see if I can get Anne Marie to let me use a computer in her office to check my email," Adrian said. "I didn't prepare to be out for an extended period of time, so there are some things I need to take care of."

Now on top of being attractive and funny, Adrian was responsible and conscientious? Be still Tate's traitorous heart.

"Help yourself to my laptop. The cabins all have pretty good Wi-Fi, so you shouldn't have a problem. It's on the desk in my bedroom, but you're welcome to bring it in here or work at the table in the living room. Wherever you're most comfortable."

Tate had a sudden image of Adrian sprawled out over the bed in his room, tanned skin standing out against the white duvet cover, dark eyes reflecting the light from Tate's laptop screen. It wasn't a sexy image—if it was, he'd probably feel less guilty. No, it was a domestic image. Homey and comfortable. Something Tate had no right to envision. Bond or no bond, he had no claim over Adrian. They were having fun right now, but Adrian was only here for a few more weeks.

The thought was more sobering than a cold shower. He was wasting time, playing at a fairy tale when he needed to be in his office meeting with a camper.

"I have to head out, but I'll be back in time for lunch. I hope you manage to get some work done today, but keep in mind that even though you have a fair amount of downtime here, you should probably take a leave of absence for the month. Work stress isn't something you should be worrying about right now."

## *Chapter Thirteen*

**LUNCH** in the mess hall was an adventure. Tate had made good on his promise to meet Adrian at the cabin and escort him to lunch, but he'd had an emergency with one of his campers and hadn't been able to stay.

He'd left Adrian adrift in a room full of foreign scents, both pleasant and unpleasant, and a million distractions. It was like eating at a crowded mall food court, though with decidedly better food.

What camp had a world-class chef? Tate had told him about that before, but Adrian assumed he'd been kidding. It was true. The camp had an honest-to-God classically trained chef who was well-known enough that even Adrian recognized him. That was saying something, considering he wasn't much of a foodie.

As if his age wasn't bad enough, he also had nothing remotely appropriate to wear. Adrian was grateful Tate had come to the rescue yet again. His clothes hadn't arrived yet, but even when they did he wouldn't have anything to wear. He'd packed for a week of corporate meetings, not yoga classes and casual days in the woods.

Tate was more muscular than him, and his T-shirt was snug through Adrian's broad shoulders but baggy everywhere else, which was definitely a *look* paired with the borrowed sweatpants he had on. Adrian didn't consider himself a clotheshorse, but he couldn't remember the last time he'd been out in public in sweatpants. Hell, he wasn't sure if he even *owned* any sweatpants. He ran in shorts and lived in slacks and chinos the rest of the time.

Even if he'd had the benefit of his own wardrobe, he was miles away from the fashion-forward teens around him. They were all wearing designer jeans and trendy shirts, which seemed like a bad idea for kids who didn't have full control over their shift. He'd lost count of how many items of clothing—Tate's clothing, mostly, which he felt guilty about—he'd ruined since the Turn, seams bursting to shreds when the shift triggered unexpectedly.

Adrian couldn't have stuck out more if he tried. That much was becoming clear the more he ventured out into the camp at large.

It was a lot like high school, or at least what he remembered of it. Adrian could easily pick out the cliques while the campers flowed around him in the mess hall, segregating themselves into small groups and laying claim to parts of the cafeteria. There were probably only thirty kids at the camp this session, but they were a perfect microcosm of werewolf society. It wasn't hard to identify the kids on the Alpha track—they moved with a confidence and self-assurance that was impossible to fake. The more aggressive kids—the ones who were the loudest, the roughest, the first to laugh at a mistake or jeer at someone a little different—all congregated together, rallying around a kid who had the posturing of an Alpha but not the natural comportment. The rest of the campers gave that table a wide berth. Then there were the campers who were quiet and frequently looked toward the table of would-be Alphas for their social cues. These would be the kids who would grow up to be the omegas, or the worker bees as Adrian jokingly called them. He used the term often at home, usually eliciting a smack upside the head from his mother but not a contradiction. Obeisance to the Alpha was part of their DNA, but these werewolves took it to the next level. While all werewolves instinctively ceded to the head of the Pack, the worker bees were almost fanatical in their Alpha worship. Frankly, it was creepy.

Adrian wasn't sure where he'd fit in with his Pack when he went home. He wasn't going to be a worker bee, that much was certain. The Turn hadn't awakened a drive to lead in him, but it hadn't sparked a drive to follow, either. He didn't feel any more connected to his Alpha or his Pack than he had as a human, and that was worrying.

Werewolves settled together in groups because there was safety in numbers, and biology hardwired them with a pack mentality to support that. Adrian's Pack was also his family, but that wasn't always the case. Sometimes all that held a Pack together was the pull of the Alpha's magnetism—something Adrian hadn't felt as a human and didn't feel now. He loved his Pack, but he didn't feel a magical connection to them like all the books said he should. Being away from his Alpha should feel like a physical weight, but all he felt was the normal amount of homesickness he experienced whenever he traveled.

He had class with Tate in a few minutes, but Adrian caught Kenya as she was on her way out of the mess hall.

"Kenya? Can I ask you a quick question?"

She stopped and gave him a kind smile. "Of course, Adrian. But if it's too involved, I reserve the right to table it until our session later. Fair?"

"Fair," he agreed. "I just—I'm supposed to feel a bond to my Pack, right? Everything I've read says being away from my Alpha should feel like a physical ache, and I overheard a couple of kids talking about it at lunch, and it sounded like they felt it. I don't, not at all." He fidgeted with a frayed thread on hem of his shirt. "Is that normal? Does it take a while to kick in or something?"

Kenya reached out and stilled his hand, stopping him from ripping the thread out of the borrowed shirt. He dropped it guiltily.

"There is no normal," she said, her voice oozing patience. Instead of soothing him like it was probably supposed to, it set Adrian's nerves on edge. He didn't want to be coddled or pandered to. He was here to learn control so he could get back to his life, not to have his hand held through any emotional blip.

"But most people feel it, right?"

"Adrian, there's no right way to be a werewolf. Maybe you won't ever connect on a deeper level with your Pack. Maybe you will, but only after you return home and have a chance to bond with them as a werewolf. Maybe—"

She cut herself off with a shake of her head, and Adrian leaned in. "Maybe *what*?"

"It's unlikely, and I don't want to freak you out."

There was literally no chance of that, not with the lead-in she'd given it. "Just tell me."

Kenya sighed. "I've read that werewolves who are moonmated have muted Pack ties because their bond with their mate is so strong." She shook her head again. "But it could be anything. Just go easy on yourself, Adrian. The truth is we don't know what's normal for you. Diann said physiologically and control-wise you're further along in your Turn than the other wolflings in your cohort. Maybe this is different too."

"If that was the case, wouldn't I have formed my attachment to my Pack earlier rather than later? If I'm on some sort of accelerated path?"

"I don't know."

Adrian wanted to be mad at her for the cop-out answer, but she was clearly frustrated by it too. It wasn't fair to blame her for not having answers—she was just as out of her depth here as he was.

"I'm sorry for badgering you. I'm just a little on edge, and I hate feeling so out of control."

"I can't even imagine. You're doing so well. I have no doubt that by the next full moon, you'll be in control and ready to go back to your life." She reached out and squeezed his shoulder. "And that isn't me blowing smoke up your ass, okay, Adrian? I mean it. And for me to be so certain, despite everything we don't know? It means I have complete confidence in you. You've got this."

Adrian swallowed past the lump in his throat and blinked rapidly, trying to dispel the tears that had welled there unexpectedly. "Thanks." A tear escaped, and he dashed it away with the back of his hand. "I don't know why I'm crying."

Kenya rubbed his back. "Hormones," she said wryly. "Frankly, I'm surprised you're as level-headed as you've been. Look around." She removed her hand from his back and gestured toward the emptying mess hall. "These wolflings are a hot mess, and unfortunately, you're one of them. Don't feel bad about the tears. It's part of the process."

He blew out a quavering breath. "Stupid process."

"The stupidest," she agreed solemnly. "Just one more bit of advice. Don't let Tate shut you out. That man has a head as hard as granite, and it's going to take someone who's every bit as stubborn as he is to get through it."

**"FIND** a seat, everyone, so we can started," Tate called out from the front of the small stadium-style lecture hall. There were only fifteen kids in the room, but it was so loud there could have been twice as many. Remembering the way he'd teased Tate earlier, Adrian took a seat in the middle of the first row, almost directly in front of the desk Tate was sitting on.

It took a few more minutes before everyone was seated and quiet, and Adrian took advantage of the time to look around. All the buildings looked pretty rustic from the outside, but the inside of every one he'd been in was state of the art. It was obvious that no expense had been spared in the camp's construction and upkeep, which made him wonder exactly how much this stay was costing him. He'd blindly signed anything they'd put in front of him when he'd arrived, exhausted from the trip and fully aware he didn't have a lot of room for negotiation. That had seemed reasonable at the time, but in the light of day, he could see that might have been a mistake. Odds were good that a night here cost more than a night at the Four Seasons.

Tate clapped his hands, and Adrian winced at the sharp sound, regretting his seat choice. Would his hearing always be this sensitive? How did people deal with that?

"Now that we're all ready to pay attention," Tate said, standing and leveling the class with a solemn look, "let's get started. I'm sure you're all wondering why I've gathered you here today—"

"Social media?" a girl from a few rows behind Adrian said, her tone confused. "It's on the syllabus."

Adrian's lips quirked into a grin when he saw Tate stifle a groan. He met Adrian's eyes for a split second, and a chill went down Adrian's spine at the playful annoyance in his gaze. Poor Tate. It must be hard to be surrounded by teenagers all the time.

"Well, that joke went over like a lead balloon," Tate said, shaking his head. "Yes, Brittany, we're talking about social media today."

Adrian turned to look up at the back row when someone scoffed loudly. "What can an old guy like *you* teach *us* about social media?"

It was pretty close to what Adrian had asked earlier, but with a knife-edge of irritation and scorn instead of playfulness. The kid was clearly trying to cause a scene, but Tate didn't take the bait. Adrian did, though. He could feel his skin start to tighten, and he tamped down on it as hard as he could, silently begging his body not to shift.

"Well, Ryan, I'm so glad you asked!" Tate said cheerfully, as if Ryan's question hadn't been dripping with condescension. Tate's easy manner made it easier for Adrian to breathe through his own annoyance, and after a moment the itchy-hot feeling subsided.

"I'm sure everyone in this room is well-versed in how to use social media, but it's my job to make sure you are using it responsibly," Tate continued.

"Who made you the dick pic police?" Ryan jeered, and this time Adrian didn't turn around. He kept his gaze trained on Tate, who aside from stiffening a little didn't outwardly react to the taunt.

"Honestly, I'm not interested in policing who you share intimate photos with," Tate said, unruffled by Ryan's disrespect. It was probably a daily occurrence around here, Adrian realized. How the hell did Tate do this every day? Adrian had spent a grand total of less than an hour out and about with these kids, and he was ready to kill them all. And he wasn't even in charge of them—he was just a bystander! Adrian couldn't imagine putting up with this kind of irritation every day.

"That is," Tate continued, "unless those photos in any way compromise the safety of werewolfdom. And even in that event, I'm not the one you have to be worried about. Your Alpha is bound by werewolf law to turn anyone who flaunts our rules and risks exposure, literally or figuratively, over to their local Tribunal." Tate arched a brow as he lifted his face to look in Ryan's direction. "I don't have firsthand experience with that, but from what I've heard it's not pleasant. And that's if your own Alpha doesn't kill you instead of handing you over for trial."

The snickering and whispers that had filled the room quieted as Tate spoke, his voice measured but firm. Adrian doubted any of these kids had witnessed a trial or punishment, but he had. In addition to being the Alpha of the Pacific Northwest, his mother also sat on the West Coast Werewolf Tribunal. Adrian was well aware of the fate rogue werewolves met, and it wasn't something he'd wish on anyone.

"That goes for *any* exposure," Tate said. He let the words hang for a moment before continuing. "Even accidental. So let's say you take a selfie at a Pack run on the full moon because your eyebrows are on fleek, or whatever the cool wolflings are saying these days, but in doing so you accidentally capture your cousin shifting in the background. That photo will land you in the same cell as a werewolf who posted a Vine of himself cleaning his claws with a cheese knife."

The class laughed, but Tate shook his head. "Both of those are true stories. You can read about the cases for tonight's homework." He handed a stack of spiral-bound books to the girl who'd taken the seat next to Adrian, and she started passing them out amid groans and growls from the class. "I want you to read the first four cases and be prepared to talk about them in class tomorrow. We'll be using this time for the rest of the week to talk about social media and how you can use it responsibly."

Tate's head shot up, and his gaze zeroed in on Ryan. "Like I said, Ryan, it isn't your penis that concerns me. It's your claws and your fur," Tate deadpanned, responding to whatever Ryan had whispered to the person sitting next to him. "Or rather, to put it in words you'd understand, I give no shits about your dick, dude. If sending pictures of your schlong to other people is what puts lead in your pencil, that's really none of my business. As long as it's your wang and not your

wolf, you won't have problems with the Tribunal."
He paused and raised an eyebrow. "Now, your Alpha
is another story. I doubt your dad would be thrilled to
know his son is sowing his virtual oats like that, but
that's between you two."

The class erupted into raucous laughter, and Adrian
could practically feel Ryan's glower from five rows
away. He was surprised to hear Tate needle the boy, but
he had to defer to Tate being the expert here. Obviously
he felt that was the way to get through to Ryan. Adrian
hoped he was right. If he wasn't mistaken, Ryan was
the son of a prominent Alpha. They could make a lot of
trouble for Tate if they wanted to.

Tate spent another twenty minutes talking about
the different social media platforms and giving a brief
overview of how each presented a unique challenge for
exposure. It wasn't a subject that interested him in the
least, but Adrian absorbed it all, enjoying the chance to
sit back and stare unabashedly at Tate.

"We're going to split up into small groups to talk
about how you'll approach using social media differently
now. Go ahead and choose your own. We won't be
reporting back to the class on this, so feel free to take
your discussions onto the grounds."

The class broke up immediately, and Adrian hesitated.
Should he go find a group to attach himself to? It wasn't
like he was dumb enough to get himself into trouble online.
He hadn't been lying when he'd told Tate he wasn't much
for social media. He was on Facebook and Twitter and he
had a Snapchat he only used to talk with a few close friends
and his siblings.

And Grindr. But it wasn't like he was going to be
putting up a profile picture of himself wolfed out or
include his new penchant for rare steaks and moonlit

strolls on all fours in his bio. Grindr was good for scratching a very specific itch, and it wasn't one that involved giving any details away other than a few photos that were skimming the lines of decency—though not the dick pics Tate had teased Ryan about earlier.

"Adrian, hang back, yeah?"

Tate's soft words had Adrian breathing a sigh of relief. He wondered if Tate actually wanted to talk to him or if he was just saving him from what promised to be an excruciating group conversation.

"I promise most of the things we'll do here will actually be beneficial," he said, his tone apologetic. "There's one large group session in the morning— Tribunal rules and werewolf politics, stuff you probably know backward and forward, given who your mom is—and the session I teach in the afternoon about werewolfing in the community. We're doing social media this week, but we'll move on to other exposure risks soon."

A thrill went through Adrian at the knowledge that he'd have this afternoon slot with Tate every day. It didn't matter what he talked about; Adrian just enjoyed sitting there and getting to drink him in.

"Please tell me Werewolfing in the Community is the official title on the syllabus that girl was talking about."

Tate flashed a toothy grin. "Brittany. She's a real stickler for the rules. There isn't a syllabus. It's more of a guidebook that lays things out for the month." He frowned. "Normally you'd have gotten one at orientation."

"But my entrance to camp was unconventional," Adrian finished for him, rolling his eyes. "No one's going to blame you for not giving me the welcome speech and the tour, Tate."

Tate flashed him an apologetic smile. "Your next class today is a small group session working on relaxation and focus with Quinn. She's great. I sit in every once in a while for a refresher because she's so good at guided meditation."

"It's not like I have anywhere else to be."

Except he did. He'd already missed a day of meetings and planning sessions back in Portland, and assuming everything went perfectly, he could still expect to miss at least a full month of work. He'd taken Tate's advice this morning and cleared his schedule indefinitely, but it wasn't like he could turn off his brain by moving some meetings around. Not to mention his frustration with the way Tate seemed to run hot and cold. Meditation sounded like a pretty good idea.

"It's weird, having so much energy but also being exhausted."

Tate hummed sympathetically. "That's normal. It's also why we recommend campers attend both the morning and evening workout sessions." He sized Adrian up with a curious look. "It's SoulCycle tonight, but if that's not your thing, Harris and I usually go for a run around dusk. You're welcome to join us if you'd rather work off some of that energy in the woods."

That brought all kinds of dirty images to Adrian's mind, and he shook them aside. "I'd like that. Assuming my clothes get here today," he said, looking down at his makeshift outfit.

Tate laughed, deep and loud. "Ah, actually, you won't need clothes. We shift and run as wolves. It's isolated enough here that as long as we stay on the property, we're safe, but going at dusk gives us an extra bit of protection from prying eyes."

Adrian flushed. Of course they'd run as wolves.

"Hey, this is a big change for you," Tate said, resting a hand on Adrian's shoulder and giving it a squeeze. "For the last eight years you've been living as a hundred percent human. Why would it occur to you that we'd shift? But don't worry. You'll integrate just fine. You just have to give yourself time."

Adrian swallowed past the lump in his throat. Yet again, his emotions were getting the best of him.

"Right." Unlike earlier, he managed to get control of himself before the actual tears started. He cleared his throat. "I do have one question, though."

"I'm all ears."

"Is werewolfdom really a word?"

Tate barked out a laugh. "This from the man who asked about Google+?"

Adrian grinned. "Google+ is a thing. Werewolfdom? Not a thing."

"What would you suggest I say? Werewolfkind?"

Adrian's mother often said *wolfdom*, but Adrian didn't like emphasizing the wolf part of their biology. It might be a throwback to his own insecurities over not manifesting the Turn when he'd become nineteen, but whatever the reason, his aversion to calling his kind wolves in any incarnation was strongly ingrained.

"Why not just call us werewolves? That's what most people say."

Tate clucked his tongue. "Because I'm trying to impart a sense of responsibility to the larger community. Yes, we're werewolves individually, but we're part of something bigger. Like humans being part of humankind. We're werewolves and we're part of werewolfdom."

Adrian pursed his lips, considering. Put like that, it sounded reasonable. "I'll accept werewolfdom, then."

"Well, as long as you approve," Tate said, bowing at the waist. He checked his watch. "I've got some time before I need to be anywhere. Want to walk over to Quinn's studio with me? I'll introduce you. Maybe I'll sit in for a few minutes. My head could use some clearing too."

Adrian had absolutely no chance of meditating with Tate near him, but he'd rather spend time with him than achieve inner Zen anyway.

"Sounds good. Lead the way!"

## *Chapter Fourteen*

*Two weeks later*

**EVEN** though he was surrounded by people, Tate had spent years living alone. He'd put in his time monitoring the campers' cabins when he'd started at Camp H.O.W.L., but that was behind him. Now someone else was the low man on the totem pole and was stuck living with an ever-revolving cast of teenage boys.

Tate liked his quiet, and he liked knowing he could do what he wanted and not worry about anyone else. He'd grown up sleeping in a dormitory along with the other boys under the age of nineteen on his father's compound, and that had meant no privacy.

Worse than no privacy, it had meant there were half a dozen spies with eyes on him at all times. If he borrowed a book from the bookmobile the library sent out from time to time, his father knew about it within the hour. He'd had to resort to making himself a nest in the hayloft, hiding there when he needed to escape or wanted a moment to himself to think or read.

He'd expected living with Adrian to be difficult, but it wasn't. And that upset him more than the thought of sharing space with someone who inconvenienced him. Adrian *didn't* inconvenience him. Not in the least. Tate liked having him there. They'd been living in each other's pockets for two weeks, and by all rights Tate should be climbing the walls—but he wasn't. He looked forward to coming back to the cabin and having someone there to talk to. The way their scents had mingled in the shared spaces was maddening, but also comforting. For the first time he could remember, the cabin felt cozy and welcoming.

They were on the same page almost across the board—when they liked to eat, what they did in their free time, balancing quiet time with time spent hanging out. Adrian had slipped into Tate's daily routine seamlessly. He was the ideal roommate, which should have been a good thing.

It wasn't. Not by a long shot. Because along with the inside jokes and comfortable companionship came smoldering looks and flirty banter that made Tate's inner wolf sing—and the rest of him shy away.

"Tell me again how it annoys you that he puts the cap back on the toothpaste," Kenya drawled, and Tate scowled at her from his place on the floor.

"Don't make it sound childish," he snapped, aware he was being incredibly juvenile even as he said it.

"It sounds to me like you're just looking for reasons the two of you aren't a good match," she said, and he threw the balled-up sock he had in one hand at her.

She caught it deftly, unfurled it, and examined it. "I was looking for that one!" she said triumphantly, matching it to one in her basket and folding them together.

"Remind me again why I agreed to help you fold your laundry?" Tate asked as he sought out more socks from the pile.

"Because you're having an existential crisis, and I told you I couldn't counsel you officially because the existential crisis is about one of my patients?"

Tate threw the unmatched socks back on the pile and lay back down, spreading out on her carpet. "It's not an existential crisis."

"It isn't," she agreed. "It's not a crisis at all. It's a good thing, and you don't know how to deal with that. You, Tate Lewis, actually don't know a good thing when it bites you in the ass, and that's partly my fault. I should have made you go out and do more things before you installed yourself here as the camp hermit."

He rolled up to his side and glared at her. "I am not the camp hermit."

"You never leave the grounds. That makes this your hermitage." She frowned. "Is that a word? Hermitude? No, that would be your hermit-y attitude. Hermitage, I'm sticking with that. We'll get you a plaque made to put outside your cabin. Tate's Hermitage."

He groaned and rubbed his hands over his face. "And you can't make me do anything, anyway. I'm my own man."

"Sure you are, sugar," she said sweetly. He didn't doubt that if they'd been close enough, she would have patted his hand. "So be your own man on this and man up and make a move!"

Tate couldn't help but smile. He'd come to Kenya because he needed someone to talk things out with, not in any sort of professional manner, but just as a friend. Kenya had been that for him for over a decade.

She'd been his advisor at IU, taking him under her wing as soon as they'd met, and she'd sussed him out as a werewolf. It could be dangerous to be an unaffiliated werewolf in a city, but that was the beauty of a college town. They existed outside of traditional territories. Kids came and went all the time, though few of them were Packless like Tate. Kenya had questioned him on that as soon as she'd realized she had a wolfling in her Intro to Psychology class his freshman year, killing his plan to fly under the radar through college.

In retrospect, it had been a stupid plan. Not just because any werewolf would be able to smell him— but also because he was fresh off his Turn, only a few months past his first shift. He needed support and help, and he sure as hell hadn't gotten any from his Pack. He knew the basics about controlling his shift because he'd figured them out on his own. Tate wouldn't have lasted two moons on a college campus stuck in a room with his clueless roommate and no place to get out and run.

Kenya had fixed all that. As soon as he'd admitted he didn't have a Pack—and as soon as she'd absorbed that and drawn her own conclusions, once she figured out who his Pack had been—she'd morphed into his mentor. She was motherly, but also a friend. He didn't know where he'd be without her. Certainly not here, lying in a pile of socks and bemoaning all his life choices. It was down to Kenya's meddling that he had a life to bemoan, and she took every opportunity to remind him of that. Surprisingly, it hadn't come up today. She was probably saving it for the coup de grace later. As killing blows went, it was a good one.

There wasn't anyone else in the world he'd feel comfortable having this conversation with—aside from Adrian, and since Adrian was currently the reason Tate was angsting harder than a Taylor Swift song, he wasn't a good choice for a confidante.

Tate was past denying that their bond was something special. Between their unnatural closeness and the way they were in sync, there was no point pretending they weren't bonded. It shouldn't matter what they called that bond, but it did. A Turn bond he could handle, but a moonmating? That was something different. What he had with Adrian wasn't the abusive, manipulative relationship Tate had grown up believing a moonmating was, but that didn't mean it was easy to forget nineteen years of conditioning. This was new territory for him. Scary territory.

"I'm just saying, can't the guy have some faults? He's the neatest houseguest ever. Yesterday he took out the trash. Even I don't take out the trash! That's what the maintenance crew is for!"

Kenya clucked her tongue. "You know they don't take out anyone else's, right?"

Tate sat up. "They don't?"

"No! They do that because they feel sorry for you because you're the camp hermit. The maintenance crew is here to take care of the grounds and clean up the public spaces. Last I checked, your cabin is not a public space."

"It is now," he muttered, flopping back down. Socks rained down on him, and he cracked one eye open to see her standing over him, emptying her basket of matched socks on his head.

"So he's perfect, and you're enjoying yourself for the first time in possibly ever," she said, her hand on her cocked hip and the basket at her other side. "And what? You're waiting for the other shoe to drop? You can't stand being with someone so perfect for you? You're...." She paused, her expression turning serious. "You're waiting for him to leave."

"He will!" Tate brushed the socks off and got to his feet. He fully acknowledged it was ridiculous for him to have abandonment issues—after all, *he'd* been the one to leave everything behind—but the mind often wasn't logical in the things it clung to. Tate shied away from attachments because he'd spent his childhood neglected and abused, and that wasn't something a person just got over.

Tate rubbed his eyes. "He has to leave. He has a life across the country. He has a family."

"He does, and you have a life here. But what kind of life is it, for either of you? I'm not breaking any confidences when I tell you Adrian is lonely. I know you know that. He's talked about it with you. He's told me as much. He's trying hard not to rush you, but he wants more than you're giving him. A few stolen kisses and conversations isn't enough to build a life on, Tate."

It was difficult to have this conversation with Kenya and not try to milk her for information about Adrian, middle-school style. Had Adrian talked about him? Of course he had. He probably talked about little else—that is, if Adrian's every waking thought was about Tate like Tate's was about him. Adrian had been open about his feelings for Tate, and Tate had been open about his discomfort with either of them having those feelings. And just like that, Adrian had dropped it.

That drove Tate crazy too. He didn't like talking about it, but he didn't like not talking about it, either. It seemed to build and grow even without his stoking it, and that more than anything scared him. There wasn't any point in kidding himself—if he had any sort of relationship with Adrian, it would be the serious sort. If what they had was actually a fledgling moonmate bond, that didn't lend itself to one-night stands or friends with benefits.

They might not say the words marriage, but the commitment would be just as real. He didn't feel capable of anything but going all in with Adrian—and that terrified him. Faced with all or nothing, his instinct was to take the nothing.

"There isn't any point," Tate said. He collapsed in the one armchair in the room that didn't currently have sweaters laid out to dry on it. "I'm not interested in something that has an expiration date."

"It doesn't have to have an expiration date," Kenya said. "Lots of people do the long-distance thing. And there are plenty of opportunities for both of you to work anywhere in the country. You could get out of here, start somewhere new. It would be good for you. You use this place as a crutch, Tate. You're never going to grow into who you were meant to be if you're hiding here."

That stung. He wasn't hiding here. He was comfortable. Settled. Finally at peace with himself. Or at least he had been before Adrian had come. Now he dreamed of a different life, one with Adrian in it. One where he actually used his degree to tangibly help people instead of just babysitting petulant rich teenagers through the Turn.

There were kids he'd reached over the years, he knew that. The counselors made a real difference for kids who came and needed their help. But those kids were few and far between. For every Ryan, there were two dozen Brittanys, kids who came because they needed to get through their Turn and learn control and otherwise viewed this as a month-long vacation.

The camp had a SoulCycle studio, for God's sake. In the middle of nowhere, Indiana. A SoulCycle studio and a Pilates reformer in a multimillion-dollar facility tucked into a forest.

His life was ridiculous.

"I can't be sure he would want that," Tate said after a long pause.

"You can't be sure Adrian would want that or you can't be sure *you* would want that?" Kenya put the basket down and came over to give him a quick, hard hug. "It's okay to not know what you want, but it's not okay to just close doors because you are afraid of what might possibly be on the other side. You two are in this together, and you owe it to Adrian to talk to him about it. Maybe you share the same fears. Maybe the thought of having a moonmate is just as terrifying to him as it is to you. Adrian is meant to be in your life, Tate. It's up to you two to decide what form that relationship takes, but when I look at the two of you, there's a lightness and a happiness in both of you that shouldn't be wasted."

Tate hung his head and took a breath. Tears stung his eyes, and he dashed them away with the back of his hand. He'd been emotional lately, more like he'd been when he'd been a lost college freshman hiding from his Pack.

Maybe Kenya wasn't the right person to be talking to right now. They shared too much history, and sometimes talking to her brought back memories he'd rather have stay buried.

"I'd have to tell him," Tate said suddenly.

"He knows," Kenya said gently, like he was some sort of agitated patient. "You had me tell him. He knows who you are, Tate. Not just who you were, but who you *are*. Adrian sees you more clearly than you see yourself."

Tate stalked to the door, his throat tight. "Finding a moonmate is a big deal."

"I know. So does Adrian. A chance to bond like that is rare, Tate. It shouldn't be wasted."

"I just—I can't be sure, you know? There are things about growing up on the compound I haven't told you about. Things that make it hard to accept that moonmates are real. To you, the bond is a chance at a fairy tale. To me, it's a reminder of how fucked-up the world can be." He shook his head and let the words lay without explanation. "I need to tell Adrian everything, even the things you don't know. I can't let things get any further with him before he knows exactly who he'd be getting involved with."

"Then do that," she said. "Have this conversation with him, not me." He looked up, and she gave him the motherly smile that always made him feel like a child who'd gotten something right. Or at least what he assumed it would feel like—affirmation had been sparse when he'd been a kid. The Pack he grew up in had been more of the "spare the rod, spoil the child" mentality.

Just another thing he needed to explain to Adrian before they could go any further. Tate's entire adult life was built on lies, and it was going to be difficult to take them apart and lay himself bare for another person.

"You are more than your past," Kenya said when he didn't respond. "And you could have an amazing future if you let yourself. Be happy, Tate. That's all any of us want for you. If that's with Adrian, then wonderful. If it's not, that's wonderful too, so long as it's what you want, not this twisted idea of what you think you deserve."

Tate's stomach rolled at her words. No matter what he did in life, what he accomplished, part of him would always be the scared little boy who hid away in the hayloft to read stolen books.

"I'll talk to him."

"Go right now, before you lose your nerve."

Tate shot her a dirty look, but she shook her head. "Oh no, sir. I know you, Tate Lewis. I know how that beautiful brain of yours works."

She had a point. Given enough time, Tate would rationalize why talking to Adrian would be a mistake and change his mind about telling him anything. It was a cycle he'd been locked in since they met.

The problem was the reasons he came up with were good ones. But so were the reasons on the other side.

"It'll have to wait until tomorrow," Tate said, looking out the window. Harris was standing outside, waiting for him. "I need a run tonight, and Adrian goes to bed pretty early."

Tate was a night owl, and Adrian said he usually was too. He was almost always sacked out by the time Tate returned from his nighttime run, probably because his body was still catching up after the exhaustion of the Turn. Tate hoped Adrian might be able to join them regularly soon—he'd only made it out twice, but Tate had enjoyed both runs immensely.

Kenya made a disappointed sound but didn't stop him from leaving. "Don't think I won't ask you after breakfast," she warned as he passed through the door.

## Chapter Fifteen

**ADRIAN** punched at his pillow, knowing it was trite and unhelpful but at a loss for what else to do. He hadn't felt this uncomfortable in his own body since puberty, which made sense. This *was* puberty, but he wasn't a wolfling of nineteen, he was a grownass man of twenty-seven, who needed to get to sleep or he'd be cranky as hell in the morning.

He'd learned to deal with his hyper senses during the day, but it was nearly impossible for him to tune things out at night. Even light coming in under the crack in his door from the hallway was enough to keep him awake, which meant he woke with the sun every morning. He'd tried to adjust by going to bed hours earlier than he usually would, but all that accomplished was adding a few hours of tossing and turning to his night.

He'd tried running with Tate and Harris to exhaust himself, since a good workout before bed usually guaranteed solid sleep for him, but running in wolf form keyed him up even more and made it impossible to drift off.

It was getting better, though. A week ago he'd have killed for the kind of sleep he was getting now, so it was probably just a matter of time before his normal sleep pattern returned. The thought of eight hours of uninterrupted sleep made him want to cry.

He definitely slept better when Tate was in the cabin, even if he was a room away. That's why he didn't mind that Tate returning from his nightly run woke him up more often than not. It was easier to get back to sleep knowing Tate was just a few dozen feet removed, and the white noise from the shower Tate took every evening helped lull Adrian back to sleep.

That hadn't worked tonight, though. Tate had been as quiet as a church mouse when he'd come in, but it had still roused Adrian from his fitful sleep. He'd lain awake listening to the shower, but instead of relaxing him like it normally did, tonight all he could think of was Tate's naked, soapy body. Water running in rivulets over the defined muscles of his arms and down the hard planes of his chest, sluicing lower and touching parts of Tate that Adrian desperately wanted to.

He and Tate had been dancing around their attraction for weeks now. And while Tate wasn't as skittish as he had in the beginning, he wasn't starting impromptu make-out sessions, either. They had great conversations, and Adrian loved being near him, but there had been exactly zero progress on the physical front since the kisses they'd shared, and it was killing him.

Adrian stared at the ceiling until the shower in the bathroom they shared shut off, the comforting noise of water morphing into the quiet sounds of Tate getting ready for bed. Adrian had almost managed to lull himself into a sleepy state when a noise startled him. He held his breath, listening for more.

"Oh shit," Tate muttered, his voice so low it was almost a growl.

Adrian hadn't keyed into Tate's heartbeat since the Turn bond had ended, but tonight it was so loud it could have been thrumming in Adrian's own chest. And once he started listening in, he couldn't escape the quiet moans and breathy exultations.

"So close. Jesus," Tate whispered.

The discomfort that had made Adrian toss and turn minutes ago eased, replaced by a different kind of bodily awareness. The cotton sheets that had felt like sandpaper now whispered over his skin like a caress. He arched off the overheated pillow, straining to hear more.

Adrian couldn't make out any sound other than Tate's small gasps and whispered words. Was he hearing what he thought he was hearing? Surely there would be the sound of skin slicking against skin, wouldn't there?

He bit his lip and held his own breath, trying his hardest to concentrate on the sounds coming from across the cabin. Try as he might, he couldn't isolate any other sounds. He'd spent the last few days trying desperately to block his extra senses, but now he was cursing himself for not exploring how to push those boundaries.

Tate was quiet for a moment but then a fresh groan broke the silence. "Stroke it! Stroke it faster. Don't slow down, goddammit!" He hissed out a breath. "Almost there!"

Adrian gave up all sense of propriety and swept his blanket aside, rising to his feet before he'd even thought the movement through. He padded on careful feet to the bathroom door, avoiding the floorboard that always squeaked.

Tate had gone quiet again, and Adrian shamelessly pressed his ear against the door. He picked up the muted *shirr* of fabric rubbing against fabric. But it sounded more like a restless shifting, not any sort of purposeful movement.

Tate whisper-growled again, and Adrian's skin heated. It felt almost like the prickle of the change coming over him, but while that always left the sensation of pins and needles along his flesh, this new sensation left only a lingering buzz of excitement. The sounds from Tate's room quieted again, and Adrian swallowed. He could—he *should*—go back to bed and forget this happened. Tate was used to living alone here in this cabin, and he'd been sweet enough to invite Adrian into his private space to save Adrian from the indignity of sleeping in a bunk room full of teenagers. He shouldn't be repaying that kindness by listening in on Tate's alone time like a lecher.

He flexed his toes, the too-tight feeling returning to his skin as his arousal cooled. He didn't want to go back to bed. He wanted to inch closer and find out exactly what Tate was doing, and not just because he was attracted to him. Tonight's eavesdropping session was the first time in days Adrian had gotten any relief from his heightened senses, and he wasn't eager to let go of the distraction.

It was a poor excuse, but it was better than nothing. Adrian eased the bathroom door open, and inched into the dark room. Tate's bedroom door appeared to be closed, so there was nothing to prevent Adrian from crossing the small space. He caught a glimpse of himself in the moonlit mirror, surprised to see his eyes were almost glowing. Another by-product of the Turn.

He crept closer, stopping short of actually touching the door. With his luck it would be slightly ajar, and he'd careen into Tate's room. Adrian could think of worse things than being sprawled out in front of Tate, but doing it unexpectedly while eavesdropping wasn't the way he wanted that particular fantasy to go down.

Adrian leaned in carefully and let his ear hover just above the surface of the door. Tate's erratic breathing was audible, but the rest of the room was quiet, much to Adrian's frustration. He was just about to press his luck and inch closer when things changed.

"That's what I'm talking about!" Tate yelled. A second later there was a loud clatter.

Adrian scrambled away from the door, his heart in his throat, shuffling backward until his hip hit the marble sink. He had to resist the urge to crouch under it like a frightened dog. His hands came up involuntarily to cover his sensitive ears, which were ringing with the sudden loud noise that had cut through the quiet.

When Adrian shifted slightly, the movement knocked a can of shaving cream off the sink, and he grimaced as it fell to the floor with a loud thunk. Or, it would have hit the floor if Adrian hadn't instinctively moved to try to slow its fall. Instead, the thunk was the sound of the can hitting the top of his foot, accompanied by his yelp of pain and surprise.

White-hot fire radiated out from the top of his foot, followed by a disturbing numbness that was almost as bad. That was hardly the worst part, though. Tate's concerned voice broke the silence a second later.

"Adrian? Are you okay? What's going on?"

Adrian bit back a curse and groped madly for an excuse for why he'd been loitering in the dark bathroom. Nothing came. His mind was blank.

A knock sounded on the door. "Hey, I can hear you breathing in there, so I know you're not dead, but you're freaking me out. Are you hurt?"

Adrian flexed his sore foot, the pain subsiding almost as quickly as it had come. "Just hurt my foot," he called back, wincing when his voice cracked.

"I'm coming in," Tate said, his tone taking on the brisk authority he used with the campers.

Adrian flailed, aware he was practically sitting on the edge of the sink but unable to move before the door opened. His foot had healed almost instantly, but the real damage was done. Tate knew he'd been hanging out in the dark bathroom like a creep.

## *Chapter Sixteen*

**TATE** stared at Adrian, blinking as his eyes adjusted to the dimness. He'd had his lights on in his room since the bright light of his laptop hurt his eyes in the dark, so opening the door into the darkened bathroom was disorienting.

He'd been braced to see Adrian in some sort of trouble, but he just seemed to be sitting in the bathroom in the dark. Maybe he was feeling nauseated? The flurry of hormonal changes that came with the Turn left a lot of people with upset stomachs and headaches. He'd felt a niggling of anxiety and panic coming from Adrian before he'd opened the door, but Tate couldn't see an immediate reason for it as he inspected Adrian and the room.

"I'm sorry to barge in, but I need to make sure you're doing okay," Tate said, taking care to telegraph his movements as he slowly walked into the room. The last thing he wanted to do was startle Adrian and make things worse.

He'd noticed Adrian had been on edge all day, but he hadn't said anything because he'd been so caught up in himself and his own problems. That had clearly been a mistake, and Tate was cursing himself for that now.

He would never have let one of his nineteen-year-old campers leave his sight while they were so tweaked, but he'd gone against his own instincts and let Adrian go off on his own because Tate had wanted space. It had been stupid and selfish, and now Adrian was paying the price, left to navigate all of the changes the Turn brings without anyone there to help.

It was Tate's fault for thinking of him as an adult, not as the baby werewolf he was. Tate couldn't bring himself to use casual, teasing terms like wolfling or pup with Adrian, not even in his thoughts. There was nothing young or half-formed about the beautiful man standing in front of him in nothing more than his boxers. Even in his confused state, Adrian was smoking hot and tempting as hell.

Tate frowned when Adrian shivered. "Are you cold?"

Wolflings usually ran hot, but he was learning there was nothing by the book about Adrian's Turn. They were in new territory here, and none of the rules seemed to apply.

Adrian didn't respond, but when his shoulders shook with another slight tremor, Tate realized his misstep. He shouldn't be asking Adrian anything right now. He needed to take charge, like he would if this were a situation with a regular camper.

"Right. I'm going to get you a blanket, and we're going to figure out what's going on with you, okay?"

Instead of turning his back on Adrian, he backed away, maintaining eye contact with him. He wasn't sure if Adrian was about to snap, but he didn't want to take any unnecessary chances. As soon as he made it through the doorway, he shot to his bed and pulled off the cashmere throw a grateful parent had given him years ago. Aside from his laptop, it was the most expensive thing he owned. It was soft as sin and felt incredible next to his skin, which made it the perfect choice to wrap a half-naked Adrian in right now. The camp laundry used unscented detergent so the linens wouldn't irritate a wolfling's sensitive nose, but right now Adrian needed comfort. The absence of scent could be as disorienting as too much scent, and Tate worried that using one of Adrian's blankets could send him further into shock—if that's what was going on.

Plus his instincts were screaming for him to scent mark Adrian, and Tate had learned to trust his gut in these situations. It rarely led him wrong when he was dealing with a wolfling in distress.

"Adrian? I'm coming back in with a blanket, and then we're going to get you moved out of the bathroom."

Adrian looked up at that, and Tate could see embarrassment written all over his face. Adrian looked more like himself, which was a good sign, but he was still shivering in the cool bathroom. Tate resisted the urge to hurry, not wanting to spook Adrian, and crossed the short distance between them. When Adrian looked at him warily but didn't move away, Tate reached around him and wrapped the cashmere throw over his shoulders. Adrian's hands came up to take the ends, clutching them to his chest as soon as Tate let go.

"I'm fine," Adrian said, his voice coming out as a croak. "There's nothing wrong with me that a dark place to hide and a jar of Nutella can't fix. Really, I'm good."

Tate narrowed his eyes as he inspected Adrian. He had been pale when Tate had first come in, but now he looked flushed. A fever, maybe? Adrian's scent was all over the place, and all Tate could feel through their bond was embarrassment.

"So you've said," Tate said, giving in to a small, relieved smile when Adrian's lips curved slightly at the heavy sarcasm. "I didn't believe you then, and I don't believe you now. Why don't you join me in my room for a moment while we figure out what's going on?"

Adrian looked like he wanted to decline, but Tate had no intention of letting that happen.

"If you don't want to talk, you can just sit with me for a bit while we watch the masters."

That sparked a little life in Adrian. He raised his head, his expression questioning. "The masters?"

"It's the Baden Masters. The first big tournament of the international curling season," Tate said as he led Adrian over to where he had his laptop sitting on a table near his bed. His concern grew when Adrian choked and flushed darker at his words. Maybe he should call Diann and have her take Adrian to the infirmary. He looked peaked, and really, there was so much they didn't know about the stress the Turn would put on an adult body. Adrian had handled everything so well thus far that Tate had stopped worrying about his physical health. He cursed himself for not being more vigilant. "Are you sure you're all right?"

Adrian looked fascinated as Tate guided him to sit on the edge of the bed. He was staring at the screen with wide eyes, his attention rapt. "You were watching… curling?"

He sounded unsure, so Tate jumped in to explain. It seemed to be a good distraction from whatever had caused Adrian's bathroom freak-out.

"They're trying to get the stone into that house, see?" Tate pointed toward the screen. "It looks like a target. The center is called the button, and it's the ultimate goal. Seems easy, right? But that granite weighs about forty pounds, and it's much harder to aim and get just the right velocity than you'd think."

Adrian made a faint noise that sounded almost like a laugh. "Curling," he repeated.

Tate nodded, encouraged that Adrian was talking. "So the guy there at the far end, behind the button, that's the skip. I guess you'd call him the team captain in other sports. He's telling the lead, the guy who's holding on to the stone, how much force to use and where to aim. And then the second and third, the other guys on the ice, will use their brooms to smooth the way for the stone and get it heading in the right direction."

Adrian started laughing in earnest then, and Tate's relief morphed back into concern. "Adrian—"

"No, no, it's fine," Adrian gasped out between laughs. "Shit." He released his death grip on the blanket and held one hand against his chest, his laughs turning into wheezes as he struggled to take in enough air.

Tate moved toward the bedside table to grab his phone. "I'll call the infirmary."

Adrian lunged toward him with more coordination and speed than Tate would have expected him to show if he was in shock, so he let Adrian wrest the phone away from him.

He drew in a deep lungful that calmed the rest of his giggles and waved Tate off. "I don't need medical help," he managed. "Mental help, maybe. But medically I'm fine."

That was hardly reassuring. Tate pulled his authority around himself like a cloak, settling himself into Dr. Lewis mode. "I'm going to need you to unpack that statement for me. How exactly did you end up in the dark hunched against the bathroom sink?"

Adrian straightened, responding to the tone of Tate's voice just as Tate had hoped he would. "It's not—I'm fine. I just meant my mind was in the gutter."

Tate let silence hang between them, hoping to draw more out of Adrian as the awkwardness grew. Adrian began to fidget.

"I mean, I heard some noises from your room and I was, uh, investigating," Adrian offered meekly.

Tate raised an eyebrow. "You were investigating noises in my room? From the sink?"

Adrian's flush returned. "I wasn't at the sink, not until just before you came in. I'd been close to your door, and then something startled me, and I ended up by the sink somehow. A loud noise."

This wasn't sounding like a psychotic break or shock, which was good. But it wasn't making any sense, either. He pressed for more details.

"You heard a loud noise while you were investigating other noises, and it took you by surprise?"

Adrian hung his head for a moment and took a deep, bolstering breath before meeting Tate's eyes. "I was trying to get to sleep, but I was really restless. I have been, lately. Just kind of itchy and miserable, I guess." He shook his head when Tate tried to get a word in. "It's normal, I know. But it's so different from how I'm used to feeling, and it's got me totally on edge. And then I picked up some noises from in here, thanks to my new super hearing," he said dryly, rolling his eyes. "And I convinced myself it was okay to be nosy and invade your privacy, so I came into the bathroom to get a better vantage point."

Tate couldn't imagine what the Turn would feel like as an adult. It had been bad enough when he'd been a teenager, but teenagers are basically hormone soup anyway, so while it had been uncomfortable and awkward, so were most things at that time. At nineteen he'd still been battling random boners and growing pains, and those had blended in with the aches, pains, and heightened senses from the Turn. It must be incredibly disconcerting to feel those as a grown man. Adrian was doing amazingly well, considering.

But what could Tate have been doing that would be so distracting? He'd been in here watching a curling match with the volume turned off.

"Vantage point?" he prompted.

"Yeah. Or whatever you'd call it for eavesdropping. I guess vantage point implies sight, and I swear I wasn't going to take it that far. I respect your decision to take things slow. I'm not going to pressure you into anything," Adrian said, chagrined. He rubbed the back of his neck, causing the blanket to fall open and expose more of his toned, gorgeous chest. He had a body that would make any werewolf proud, which was all the more impressive because he'd gotten those rangy muscles as a human. Tate wondered if Adrian would fill out a bit more now and take on the more muscled physique most adult male werewolves developed or if he'd stay lightly muscled and compact.

"What could you hear?" Tate asked, curious.

"Ah," Adrian hedged. "Your breathing and heart rate were fast, and you were, uh, talking."

Tate was used to living by himself, but he'd been mindful of the fact that Adrian was just one room away tonight. And he didn't think he talked to himself, did he?

"About the game, I guess," Adrian said, his tone embarrassed. "But, uh, I thought it could be something else. And I wanted to find out for sure, because apparently either the Turn or this weird bond we share has made me into a creep as well as a slavering wolf beast."

Tate laughed. "One, you're not a slavering wolf beast. You're a werewolf. A man who can turn into a wolf by his own will, which is pretty damn cool. I know it doesn't seem like it now, but you *will* gain control."

Adrian was still leaking pheromones all over the place, which had Tate on edge himself. As his fear and anxiety receded, it was impossible to ignore the arousal he was broadcasting. Tate couldn't tamp down his own response, no matter how hard he tried. How mortifying to be lecturing Adrian on control when Tate could barely control himself. He'd never felt attraction like this to anyone else. He could barely think straight.

"And two?" Adrian prompted, his head tilted quizzically.

Tate tried to ignore the way the gesture made Adrian look even more kissable. "Two?"

"You said one, so I assumed there was a second point."

It had been easier to keep a lid on his libido when Adrian had been pale and shocky. Now his cheeks had a rosy cast to them, and his eyes were sparkling with amusement, and Tate was so, so screwed.

"Uh," he murmured, glancing away from Adrian to try to compose himself. "Two, you're not a creep. You're getting used to your new senses. You can't be blamed for letting your curiosity get the best of you."

Adrian shook his head ruefully. "Thanks for trying to give me a pass, but super senses or not, I didn't have the right to invade your privacy."

"That's just it, though. Your senses are on overdrive. Everything is hyped up right now after the Turn. Your brain is trying to figure out how to process all the extra input it's getting, and that has some side effects, like distractibility, irritability—"

"Curiosity?" Adrian interrupted, his tone dry. "Sorry, but I'm going to have to call bullshit on that one. I totally agree my brain is struggling to catch up, and it's definitely giving me problems with my attention span and making me cranky. But it's not increasing my curiosity or any other *ity* you're planning to throw in there to make me feel better. The only one that matters is *responsibility.* As in, I'm a big boy. I can take responsibility for my actions, especially when I've done something that sucks, like listening outside your door because I thought you were jacking off and I wanted to hear more."

Tate swallowed hard. The thought of Adrian listening to him getting off was making him *want* to get off. The fact that Adrian was standing in front of him wearing next to nothing wasn't helping, either.

"Oh," he said, the word coming out breathy and off.

Adrian looked up, his eyes widening as he studied Tate. Tate could imagine what Adrian was seeing. Flushed cheeks, rapid breathing, dilating pupils—pretty much the mirror image of what Tate was watching happen to Adrian.

Was this their natural attraction, or was this simply another symptom of the bond amplifying their emotions? Damned if Tate knew, and the longer Adrian stood there tempting him, the less he cared.

"Tate," Adrian said, hesitant. "If you want me to leave...."

He should. But he didn't. "I don't."

Adrian licked his lower lip, and Tate tracked the motion with hungry eyes. His pulse jumped, and the semi he'd sprung when Adrian admitted he'd wanted to listen to Tate jacking off fattened.

Adrian stepped forward, eyes still on Tate's, until they were close enough for their breath to mingle. Tate took the lead then, tilting his head and leaning forward the few millimeters that separated them.

Adrian melted against him and Tate sank into the kiss, his world narrowing to the feel of Adrian's full lips and the heat of Adrian's naked chest against his with only Tate's thin cotton T-shirt between them. The cashmere blanket dropped to the floor with a whispery sound when Adrian wrapped his arms around Tate's shoulders and pulled him even closer, their bodies touching from mouth to thigh.

Tate wasn't a monk by any means, but he wasn't out prowling the bars every weekend, either. To say he was in a dry spell would be charitable, given that Tate couldn't remember the last time he'd been in this position. His entire body felt electrified, and the world narrowed to the feel of Adrian's body against his. Forget his dry spell—he'd never felt like this before period. Full fucking stop. His brain couldn't even come up with the words to explain how different a simple kiss from Adrian felt.

Tate nudged his thigh between Adrian's legs, a thrill running up his spine at how the move brought them even closer. The need to eliminate any barrier between them thrummed like a wild thing in the back of Tate's mind, and when Adrian shifted his hips and curved his leg around Tate's calf, the dull roar of lust and need drowned out Tate's thoughts.

For a few precious seconds, nothing existed except the two of them. Their breathing synced, and the heartbeat thundering against Tate's chest matched up with his own racing pulse. They were one, joined at the lips and wrapped around each other like vines.

And then Tate felt a wave of anxiety that wasn't his crash over him, dripping icy fingers of fear through his arousal, making his breath stutter. A moment later, Adrian's nails scored Tate's shoulders where he'd been clutching him.

Adrian stumbled backward, and Tate tried to follow, desperate to maintain their link, only to stop dead when he saw the blind fear in Adrian's eyes as he looked down at his own hands, which had started to shift. Adrian's expression was wild, and he looked like he was about to bolt.

"Whoa, hey," Tate said, catching Adrian by the wrists. "Hey. Breathe. Don't fight it. Shift if you need to."

"Don't want to," Adrian bit out past clenched teeth that were lengthening into fangs.

"Okay then," Tate said, doing his best to bring his own heartrate down so Adrian might follow suit. "Close your eyes. Find three sounds to focus on. Got 'em?"

Adrian nodded tightly.

"Now find two smells you can identify."

Adrian drew in a deep breath, and Tate breathed with him. The sour tang of Adrian's fear still saturated the air, but it wasn't as sharp as it had been moments ago.

"Good. Now open your eyes and find one thing to look at."

Adrian's eyes blinked open and he stared at Tate's face, his gaze downcast. It took Tate a second to realize he was staring at Tate's lips. He wondered if they were as kiss-swollen as Adrian's were. He shook off the thought and focused on Adrian's slowing heartbeat. His claws and fangs were receding, but he still looked strung out and upset.

"You did so well," Tate crooned, talking to him like he would a wolfling during the Turn. "So well. You pulled it back and didn't shift."

Adrian tugged his arms out of Tate's loose grasp and frowned. "But I almost did."

"And if you had, there would be nothing wrong with it. That's why you're here, Adrian. To gain control over your shift. It's natural to feel the urge to shift when you're experiencing a strong emotion."

Adrian scoffed. "Wanting to fuck your brains out is a 'strong emotion' now, is it?"

A fresh wave of arousal swept down Tate's spine at Adrian's words. Even through the sarcasm, he could feel the truth in them. And he wanted the same. But now wasn't the time. Hell, he wasn't sure if there would *ever* be a time.

"Sure is," he said easily. "But I'm glad we stopped. We're going slow, remember?"

"Glacially slow," Adrian muttered.

Tate was relieved to see Adrian's sass returning. "Let's get you back to bed, and we'll talk tomorrow."

## *Chapter Seventeen*

**ADRIAN** hesitated outside Harris's office door, debating whether or not to knock. He could call home and talk to one of his brothers about this. Or he could even swallow his pride and talk to Kenya. He flashed back to his cringe-worthy sex-ed class and shook his head. No, he needed to talk to a guy for this, and Harris was the only one he knew aside from Blake—the yoga instructor—and Tate.

He took a breath and rapped on the doorframe, opening the levered handle when he heard Harris invite him in.

"Adrian, hey," Harris said, clearly surprised by the visit. "Are you looking for Tate? His office—"

"Is on the other side of camp, I know," Adrian said. "Actually, I was looking for you. I was wondering if you had some time to talk."

Harris closed the folder he'd been studying and sat up, pinning Adrian with a curious gaze. "I was just catching up on my daily reports."

"If I'm interrupting, I can go," Adrian said quickly. The bravado he'd used to get himself through the door was fading, and only embarrassment and shame were left in its wake.

"Not at all. If anything you're saving me from mind-numbing boredom." Harris's smile seemed genuine, and Adrian relaxed a tiny bit. "Come on in and shut the door behind you. Whatever's on your mind looks like a conversation best had in private."

Adrian usually had a fairly good poker face, so the fact that Harris could see through his smile either meant Harris was really good at his job or Adrian was slipping. Maybe both.

"Have you talked to Tate today?" he asked without preamble. In the time he'd been at the camp, he hadn't seen Tate spend time with anyone outside of official business, aside from Kenya and Diann. Everyone was cordial to him, but Tate didn't seem to have many friends among the staff.

Harris's brows furrowed. "Today? No. We have an all-staff meeting on Thursdays, so I'll see him tomorrow. Is there a problem? Are you not getting along? He can be a lot to take sometimes, but he's a good guy. Secretive as hell and quiet, but a good guy."

Adrian had experienced the secretive part, but not the quiet. Distressed as he was, it made him feel warm inside to know Tate felt comfortable talking with him.

Adrian blew out a breath he hadn't realized he'd been holding. "Yes, but I'm the problem, not him." He scratched the back of his neck, uncomfortable and not sure where to start. It was probably better to just go for it. "We were, uh, getting intimate—" He raised his gaze from the carpet to Harris's face, but he didn't see any judgment there. It gave him the courage to continue. "—and things were getting, uh, involved, when all of the sudden…."

He trailed off, too mortified to continue. But luckily he didn't have to. Harris made a sympathetic noise and nodded.

"You lost control and shifted." He just shrugged when Adrian made a strangled sound of agreement. "It happens. You may be an adult, Adrian, but in wolfling terms, you're a baby. A fresh Turn. From what I've heard, you've been working your ass off in your classes and taking all the sessions seriously. But it doesn't happen overnight. You're doing all the right things. You just have to give it time."

Adrian was getting sick of that refrain. He understood, but it was still frustrating not to be in control of himself no matter how hard he worked at it.

"But is it normal to shift then? I mean, I've had it happen when something startled me or when I get angry, but during sex? Really?"

Harris grinned. "Any strong emotion can trigger a shift before you have control. Mad props on that, by the way. Tate's been happier than I've ever seen him."

"Thanks," he said, flushing.

"So I can't imagine Tate didn't tell you shifting was normal, so why are you here? Did you want a second opinion?"

Adrian looked away.

"Cut yourself some slack, Adrian. There are going to be fuckups."

His bluntness surprised a laugh out of Adrian. "Is that the advice you give all the wolflings?"

Harris snorted. "With different language? Yes. But I figured you'd appreciate it if I just cut to the chase."

Adrian felt lighter than he had since he'd bolted from Tate's cabin. "I do."

"Good." Harris checked his watch. "If you're not ready to go face Tate yet, Blake's got a class soon you might enjoy."

He wasn't, and Adrian was grateful Harris saw that and gave him an out. He just wished it wasn't Blake's morning yoga class.

"I wouldn't go so far as to use the word enjoy," Adrian said, wrinkling his nose. "He has us chant through some of the positions, which is weird. But it would be good to work off some of this energy. I feel like I'm amped up to an eleven all the time now."

"Ah, to be young again," Harris said with mock wistfulness.

"I'm older than you," Adrian said flatly.

"Doesn't count," Harris said. "You're a new Turn. A mere tot. A babe in the woods."

"I'm closer to AARP than those woods," Adrian said, shaking his head. "Thanks for talking me down."

Harris waved him off. "I didn't do anything. You just needed someone to listen. I'm here anytime you need to talk. Unless it's about hot sex with Tate, because there are some things better left to the imagination."

Adrian's imagination had been experiencing it on overdrive all morning, remembering how a simple kiss had brought all his nerve endings alive and sent him up in flames.

"No worries on that front," he said as he headed out the door. "Old fogies like me don't kiss and tell like you young 'uns."

**ADRIAN** wanted go see Tate as soon as yoga class was over, but he was soaked with sweat after an hour in Blake's overheated studio. Hot yoga was torture in any setting, but in a studio that overlooked a serene pond filled with clear, cold water? Brutal.

The poses and heat had taken him out of his own head for a bit, though, which had been the entire point. He didn't believe in the crap Blake spewed about sweating out his negative energies, but he'd definitely achieved more inner peace while struggling not to let his sweaty feet slip off his mat during downward dog.

Adrian grimaced as his T-shirt shifted, the wet fabric sticking to his back. New plan. Head back to the cabin to shower and change, and then he could find Tate. Heat flared up his spine—in a good way, this time—as he thought about resuming where they'd left off the night before. Now that he knew arousal could spark the shift, he could be on guard for it and control it, like he'd dialed back his shift at the end of yoga when Blake rang a gong unexpectedly. Half the class had ended up furry after that, which had been the point.

Everything about the camp and classes was structured to teach wolflings control and then press them into stressful or surprising situations to test them. In hindsight, Adrian was pretty sure that was why there was such a lenient policy about wolflings sneaking out of their cabins to hook up after hours—better to have an unintended shift during sex here than with a human later.

Adrian's skin went cold under his sweat-soaked shirt at the thought of being in that situation with a stranger. Not the unexpected shifting, but the sex. He'd known Tate for all of two weeks, and he couldn't see a future with anyone but him. That was far more terrifying than the possibility of growing claws and fangs every time he popped a boner. How would a relationship with Tate work? Tate's prickliness was actually the least of their problems. They practically lived on opposite sides of the country. Adrian was part of a Pack, and Tate was Packless—and militantly so. Adrian couldn't see Tate joining his mother's Pack, but even worse, he couldn't see *himself* joining it without Tate. It was a mess.

He rolled his shoulders, relishing the burn of overused muscles. He'd take a hot shower, grab something to eat, and hopefully somewhere along the way he'd find the balls to go have a frank discussion with Tate about this moonmate bond. Tate knew a lot more about werewolves than he did, so maybe Tate could shed some light on it. Adrian only knew the basics, and even that was from gossip and family stories that had been passed down. Moonmates hadn't been included in the werewolf sex-ed class he'd taken as a teenager.

Though come to think of it, neither had shifting during foreplay. Or at least he didn't think it had. Like most of his teenage experiences, the class was blessedly a blur.

Adrian stripped off his shirt in the living room and hop-stepped out of his pants the minute he was behind closed doors in his bedroom. The clammy feel of drying sweat always made him feel disgusting.

He opened the door to the bathroom and stopped short, stunned at the sight of Tate standing at the sink wrapped in only a towel.

"Oh my God," Adrian yelped. He hadn't bothered to knock because he thought Tate would be wrapped up in therapy sessions until later. "I'm so sorry."

He backed out of the room and shut the door, his face flaming hot and his pulse racing. He hadn't seen anything indecent—or at least, it *shouldn't* have been indecent. But this was Tate, and any glimpse of skin was enough to send Adrian into hyperdrive. And seeing Tate naked while only in boxers himself? Not an ideal situation.

A second later the door flew open, and Tate hurried into the room. "Are you all right? Did you need something?"

Adrian kept his gaze on the wall over Tate's shoulder. "Other than for you to put on some clothes?"

Tate laughed. "I don't mind you seeing me like this."

"I don't mind either—that's the issue," Adrian said, his voice strangled.

Tate came closer until Adrian could look him in the eye without getting an eyeful of smooth skin pebbled with water.

"Hey," he said, reaching out and taking both of Adrian's hands in his. "Last night? That was a totally normal reaction."

Adrian swallowed and looked away. "I know that now," he said sheepishly. "But I freaked out, and I'm sorry."

"You didn't mess up, Adrian. You were confused and startled by your shift. You have nothing to apologize for. But the fact that you did? That's huge for me, Adrian. I don't have a lot of people in my life who would do that."

Guilt roiled through Adrian's gut. Tate forgiving him so easily only made him feel worse. "I was embarrassed," he said with a self-deprecating laugh. "It's kind of mortifying to be the guy who sprouts fangs and a tail when things start to get interesting with their moonmate."

Tate didn't immediately recoil from the word, which gave Adrian hope. "Better that it happen with your moonmate than someone else," he said, his voice roughening. "Better that it be *me* than anyone else."

Adrian suddenly felt shy. They'd been dancing around each other for weeks, and he felt more connected to Tate than he'd ever felt to anyone, so it didn't make sense for his stomach to suddenly be full of butterflies at hearing the word *moonmate* fall from Tate's lips. A lot about the situation they were in didn't make any sense, though. "I'd be happier if it didn't happen at all, but I'm glad it was with you too."

Adrian tilted his head and went in for a kiss, ready to pick up where they'd left off last night, but Tate backed up and dropped Adrian's hands. Disappointment stuttered through Adrian. He'd thought they were finally getting somewhere.

"I need to talk to you before we go any further. If you're my moonmate, there are things you need to know about me and my family."

"I don't need to know anything else about your family. You cut all ties with them, Tate. They aren't part of you anymore."

Tate shook his head. "They'll always be a part of me, whether I want them to be or not. And if we're together, they'll be part of you too. How do you think your Alpha will react when she finds out who I am?"

Anger erased the hurt and rejection that had settled heavy in Adrian's chest. Even though he'd had the same thought earlier, he bristled at the slam. He might not feel a connection to them, but they were his Pack. And even if that changed, they were his family. They wouldn't turn their back on him. "My *mother* will be happy I've found my moonmate. It won't matter to her what your history is."

Tate's eyes were clear and his expression unruffled when he answered. "Your *Alpha*," he said, stressing the word, "sits on the Werewolf Tribunal. The organization that has gone on record as saying my father's Pack needs to be investigated for the way it chooses to live. You really think she's going to welcome that Alpha's son into her family?"

"You renounced your Pack. You even changed your name!"

Tate nodded again, and Adrian found his calmness infuriating. "And when she asks me to tell the Tribunal where my father's compound is and I refuse, what then?"

Adrian's fury deflated. He wanted to be able to say she'd never put Tate in that position, but he knew that was a lie. His mother took her position on the Tribunal seriously, and Tate's former Pack was a big issue. She absolutely would put him on the spot, and she'd refuse to take no for an answer.

"See? It's not just who my family is, either. I'm Packless, Adrian. There's a huge stigma against werewolves like me."

"But you wouldn't have to be Packless anymore." Adrian regretted the words as soon as he'd blurted them out. Tate's expression hardened.

"I have no interest in joining a Pack. Any Pack." Tate frowned. "Even yours."

Adrian had suspected as much, but it was still hard to hear. "Fair enough."

The lines around Tate's mouth softened. "That's going to be a problem for your mother too. Being with me is going to cause a lot of problems for you, Adrian.

And not just because of that," he said in a rush when Adrian opened his mouth to respond. "There are things you don't know about my Pack. Things I've never trusted anyone enough to talk about." Tate looked down at himself and grimaced. "I'm not having this conversation in a towel."

Given what they'd already discussed while the towel wasn't an issue, that didn't bode well for Adrian. The dread that had been growing in his stomach multiplied. "I'll wait for you in the living room."

Tate disappeared back into the bathroom and Adrian tugged on a pair of shorts and a shirt. The temptation to keep walking straight out the cabin's front door and avoid whatever conversation was coming was strong, but he wouldn't do that to Tate. What was Tate so afraid to tell him? Adrian pulled his phone out of his pocket and shot off a text to his sister.

*Hypothetically, if I told you I'd met my moonmate, what would you say?*

He sat on the couch to stop himself from pacing, but he was too nervous to be still. He jiggled his leg while he waited for Tate, whose bedroom door remained closed. His phone dinged.

*Um, other than call you a cradle robber?*

Adrian barked out a laugh.

*Get your mind out of the gutter. He's 32. Technically he would be the cradle robber in this situation, not me.*

He hadn't told his sister or anyone else back home how close he and Tate had grown, and he realized now he'd been hiding him. Just as Tate thought he would. Not because he was worried about what his family would think of Tate, but because he wanted to sort out his own muddled feelings first. Texting Eliza was a big step. He was all in on this, no matter what Tate came through that door and said.

*That doesn't sound very hypothetical.*

He started to reply but then a barrage of texts came in.

*HOLY SHIT ADRIAN*

*Moonmate? For real? Those are actually a thing?!?*

Adrian blew out a relieved breath. That was exactly the response he'd been hoping his sister would have. Tate's door creaked open, and Adrian looked up to see him standing on the threshold. His hair was spiky where he'd pulled his shirt on without fixing it, and he looked sad and lost.

*Gotta go. Details later. DO NOT TELL MOM.*

She would, of course. It would save Adrian the trouble, but by telling her not to, he could take the moral high ground about it later if everything went to shit with his family.

## *Chapter Eighteen*

**ADRIAN** had been furiously texting with someone when Tate had opened the door, but he stood up and shoved his phone in his pocket as soon as Tate came in. It pinged again, but Adrian ignored it.

"No matter what you have to tell me, it's not going to change how I feel about you. We're moonmates, Tate. That's… I don't know. Biology? Fate? But we're more than that. I don't want you just because my instincts tell me you're my mate. I want you because you're funny and warm and attractive as hell. It's not just the bond, Tate."

Tate had worked himself into a frenzy of worry while he'd gotten dressed, convinced Adrian would run off again. Opening the door and seeing an empty living room would have been a bad blow.

Adrian's rant was exactly what he needed to hear.

"My father is a polygamist," Tate said. Best to dive straight in. Rip the Band-Aid off in one go. "My mother was one of his five moonmates. He's probably taken more since I left. Hell, maybe he married the girl he'd picked out as my moonmate right after my Turn."

Adrian's mouth opened, but Tate pushed on. He needed to get this all out before he lost his nerve. "I didn't think moonmates were real. Shit, I'm still not sure. But I do know that when I walked into your hospital room, the aching emptiness I've lived with for my entire life went away. I can't describe how terrifying that was. It was like a piece of me was missing. A piece I hated, but it was still like losing a limb."

He started to pace, full of nervous energy and desperate not to have to watch Adrian as all of this sank in.

"I've always dealt with my past by suppressing it. Not in an unhealthy way, or at least, not most of the time. But by not dwelling on it and instead focusing on who I am now. But when I realized we could be moonmates—for real, not the mindfuck version my father uses to brainwash his wives--it brought everything back. All the negative emotions from my childhood, all the fear and disgust."

He forced himself to stop and look at Adrian. "My father was an abusive asshole who used the fairy tale of moonmating to convince young women they were destined to be with him. So not only did I not believe in moonmates, I didn't believe in love. I couldn't ever imagine attaching myself to another person—until I met you. And I realize now that love isn't about shackling yourself to someone, it's about sharing yourself with someone. And if you're still willing to do that after everything I've just dumped on you, then I'm willing to try too."

He was a bit surprised Adrian hadn't recoiled in horror. Whenever Tate had envisioned telling someone about his childhood and the environment he grew up in, he'd imagined shock and condemnation. Not the soft look Adrian was giving him now.

"So, yeah," Tate said, winding down. "That's my big dark secret."

Adrian broke into a goofy grin. "You love me. You accept our moonmate bond."

Tate scratched the back of his neck, uncomfortable. "I do, but that wasn't the point."

"That was the entire point," Adrian said. "Everything else is important because it's part of your story, but it's not *our* story. Our story started with the most gorgeous man I've ever seen walking into a hospital room when I was scraped up, dirty, and wearing an assless gown. And he looked at me and found something he hadn't known he was missing. That's a hell of a thing, Tate."

Huh. Put like that, it kind of was.

"That's one of the things I love about you," Tate said, grinning when the word made Adrian's cheeks flush a pretty pink. "You have this optimism about the world that stuns me."

"Well, moonmates *are* supposed to be the perfect complement to each other," Adrian said with a sly smile.

"I think that was an insult, but I'm going to let it go." Tate was bubbling over with happiness. He'd literally never felt like this before. It wasn't like all of his problems had just vanished. They hadn't. But there was a lightness to the burden that hadn't been there a minute ago. Maybe this was what sharing the load felt like. That was what a moonmate was for, after all. To strengthen you and support you.

A loud banging at his door ruined the moment, and Tate stalked over to it and whipped the door open, ready to take a chunk out of whoever was on the other side. He pulled up short when he saw Kenya's worried face.

"Ryan's gone."

"What do you mean, gone?"

"I mean *gone*. His bunk is empty. He took his luggage. No one knows where he went, but the security camera footage shows him leaving by the front gate and walking off."

Tate silently cursed Ryan's timing. He turned to apologize to Adrian. "I have to go. Stay here and I'll—"

"I'm going with you." Adrian had already put his shoes on. He handed Tate a pair of tennis shoes.

That's all he needed—two wolflings on the loose. "You aren't ready to leave camp yet. Besides, I don't know what kind of mess we're going to find, and I don't want you caught up in it."

"You don't know what kind of mess you're going to find, which is exactly why you need me there. I'm the head of marketing for a multinational company, Tate. I can talk my way out of anything. If we find him and he's in some sort of trouble, we're going to need to be able to think on our feet and spin some sort of story. I'm ready. I can do this."

This take-charge Adrian wasn't one Tate had seen before, and he liked him. Adrian was usually so easygoing—hearing some steel in his voice sent an inappropriate shiver down Tate's spine. He filed that away as something to explore later, because right now they had a distressed teenage werewolf on the lam.

Tate studied Adrian, taking in the set of his jaw and the stiffness of his shoulders. He wasn't going to back down. Maybe he was right. Maybe he was ready.

"Think of it as a Werewolfing in the Community field trip," Adrian said, and Tate couldn't help but crack a smile.

"Fine." He turned to Kenya. "Who else is out looking?"

"Harris has taken a van and headed toward Bloomington. We think he might try to hitch a ride, and that's the direction that makes the most sense. Liam took another car the opposite way, toward Columbus. He's probably heading to an airport."

Tate was sure that's exactly where Ryan would go. He also knew exactly how he'd get there.

"Let's go," he said to Adrian, grabbing his keys off the rack near the door. "I'll call when we have him. Has his Alpha been notified?"

Kenya nodded, and Tate cursed. Having his father breathing down his neck wasn't going to help Ryan. If anything, it was going to make things worse.

"Anne Marie is handling that. You just go bring him back safely."

Adrian and Tate took off for the parking lot at a jog, leaving Kenya at the cabin.

"You know where he is, don't you?" Adrian asked, his breath coming in puffs as Tate pushed their speed.

There was a 90 percent chance of it. "The parking lot of the feed store about five miles from here," he said. He unlocked his car and slid in, motioning for Adrian to do the same.

Adrian shot him a puzzled look. "And why would he be in the parking lot of a feed store?"

Tate grinned. "Because that's where Wade picks up his Uber clients in town."

## *Chapter Nineteen*

**ADRIAN** had been out for a few runs in the forest surrounding the camp, but he'd been too preoccupied with running as a wolf to take much notice of his surroundings. He was enraptured by them now, though.

The drive to the feed store took them along a winding road set in the lush landscape of the Hoosier National Forest. It was early enough that most of the trees were still green, but a few early adopters had started turning vibrant yellows and reds. Adrian felt a pang of regret that he wouldn't be here in a few weeks to see the forest in its full fall glory.

Adrian was disappointed when Tate pulled off into a mostly empty gravel parking lot. A monstrosity of a building with corrugated steel siding that made it look like an oversize shed loomed across the way. A fence of rough-hewn logs lined the edge of the lot nearest the store, and Ryan sat perched on one of them, his duffel bag at his feet.

The gravel crunched under the tires as Tate rolled to a stop a few feet away from him.

Tate got out and leaned casually against the hood. "Waiting for your Uber?"

Ryan's jaw was set angrily. "You can't stop me."

"Nope," Tate agreed easily. "But you probably want to consult your Alpha before you get on a plane."

The color drained out of Ryan's face. "You didn't call him, did you?" He hopped off the fence post and grabbed Tate's arm. "Did you?"

Sweat popped up across Ryan's brow, and his hair started to lengthen. He was going to shift right here next to the wide selection of John Deere riding lawn mowers. A mountain of hay bales occupied the corner of the parking lot, and Adrian grabbed both Tate and Ryan by the arms and tugged them toward it. That way they'd at least have some cover if Ryan lost control.

"Hey, it's okay," he said. "We're going to move this over here for some privacy, okay?"

Ryan went without protest, but the change of location didn't stop the way his hair and nails were growing.

"They had to let him know because he's worried about your safety," Tate said when they'd reached the hay. "It isn't safe for you to be in public yet. They didn't call him as an Alpha, they called him as a parent."

"There isn't a difference," Ryan sneered.

*Ah.* So Ryan's angle was disaffected son of an Alpha? This was right up Adrian's alley. He raised an eyebrow at Tate, who shrugged. Adrian took that as a sign it was okay for him to take over.

"Honestly? You're probably right," Adrian said. His frankness made Ryan stop pacing and make eye contact, which was a good sign. He could still stop his shift if Adrian could get him to calm down.

"Most people don't understand how hard it is to be an Alpha's kid. Everyone's always watching you, waiting for you to screw up. And when you do, your dad comes down on you because he's embarrassed. Or at least that's what happens with my mom. She's a big deal even among Alphas. It kind of sucks."

Ryan kicked a pile of loose hay, sending dust swirling around them. It tickled at Adrian's nose and made him want to cough. He didn't, fighting to keep his features relaxed and neutral when what he really wanted to do was turn away and sneeze. Even something as benign as that could startle Ryan into a full shift.

"I can name like ten kids off the top of my head who would kill to be me. I don't know why." He kicked another pile and crossed his arms. "Even *I* don't want to be me."

That was heavier than anything Adrian was equipped to deal with, but Tate wasn't rushing to step in and take over, so he must think things were going well. "I get it. Me? I didn't Turn when I was nineteen. That's why I'm here now, because it happened after all that time. But I had almost a decade of seeing the flash of disappointment in my mother's eye every time she looked at me. And the gossip in the Pack, Jesus. I stopped going to Pack functions because I was tired of all the staring and whispering."

Ryan's lower lip trembled and he hugged himself tighter with his arms. The hair that had been thickening along Ryan's sideburns started to thin out, which was a good sign.

"God, he'd have flipped his shit if I didn't Turn." Ryan shook his head. "It's bad enough that I can't get my act together and learn control." He huffed out a bitter laugh. "He told the Pack I did so well the camp asked me to stay for another month as a counselor. Supportive, right? Like they didn't all see through that."

Adrian had no idea what to say to that. His situation was different. His mother was a crappy Alpha for him, but a good mom. He never doubted she supported him, even when she was disappointed in him.

Adrian cast a helpless look at Tate, who flashed him a brief, brilliant smile before stepping in.

"Your worth isn't tied to what your father or your Pack thinks of you, Ryan. The only person in this world whose happiness you're responsible for is yours."

Ryan swiped at his eyes angrily, and Adrian was relieved to see his claws had retracted. He didn't look like an out-of-control wolfling anymore—he just looked like a heartbroken kid. "I'm not happy, so apparently I can't even get *that* right."

"How could you be happy when you're trying to live up to standards that aren't yours?" Tate's voice was gentle and soothing. He must be an incredible therapist, Adrian realized. He clearly loved helping people—he was more animated and at ease than Adrian had ever seen him. He'd heard the phrase "in your element" before, but he'd never fully understood it until now. Tate wasn't just *in* his element—this *was* his element. This was where he could escape everything that plagued him and be Dr. Lewis instead of Tate.

Helping troubled werewolves gave Tate peace professionally, and Adrian wanted to help Tate find that in his personal life too.

Ryan's eyes were wet and his breath stuttered, but he squared his shoulders and seemed to stand taller. "I don't want to get a degree in accounting and go into business with my dad like my brothers did. I was supposed to have all year to work it out, but he called this morning to tell me he'd gotten my acceptance at Hofstra deferred so I could start in January since I was missing classes. I didn't even know he'd applied to schools for me—he didn't say anything, and I stupidly thought that meant he was listening for once."

Ryan started pacing again, his voice becoming more strained. "I never learn. He tells me that all the time, but it's true. I keep expecting something different."

"Like Charlie Brown and the football," Tate murmured, shaking his head. "We can't change our past decisions, but we can let them inform our future ones. So take the life lesson and move on. You don't have to start school in January if you don't want to, Ryan. You're legally an adult. You can choose your own path. That doesn't mean you shouldn't listen to those who are giving you guidance, but you ultimately are the one who has to live with your decision."

"He'll cut me off."

"He might," Tate said. "And you'll need to be prepared for that. But I can tell you there are far worse things. You're a strong guy, Ryan. If that happens you'll dust yourself off and start over. But don't write your family and your Pack off just yet. You need to sit down and have a serious discussion with them. They might surprise you."

Ryan blew out a breath. "How much trouble am I in for leaving?"

Tate raised an eyebrow. "Did you shift or tell anyone you were a werewolf on the way here?"

Ryan recoiled. "No! Of course not!"

"Then none," Tate said with a wink. "You didn't do anything wrong. You're free to leave the camp whenever you want if you can control yourself. And you did."

Ryan looked down at his hands, flexing his fingers and staring at them like he'd never seen them before. "I started to shift," he said, his voice full of wonder.

"And then you stopped it," Adrian said. "You pulled back. You figured it out, Ryan."

Ryan met Adrian's gaze, his lips curving into a smile so genuine it made Adrian's heart ache.

"What now?" Ryan asked, looking at Tate.

"Now you get to choose. Am I taking you back to camp or to the airport? I'm afraid your Uber has been and gone. I heard Wade's death trap rattle up about twenty minutes ago, and he left pretty soon after that."

Ryan was quiet for a moment. "I want to go back to camp. I don't think I'm ready to be out there yet."

"That? That was a responsible choice, my friend," Tate said, clapping a blushing Ryan on the back. "You're already knocking this adulting thing out of the park."

**GETTING** Ryan settled back into the camp took most of the afternoon, and it wasn't until after dinner that Adrian found himself alone with Tate again. He felt the same spark of excitement being near him, but now there was more.

He'd gotten to see something private today, and it only made him more certain what he felt for Tate really could become love. The moonmate bond brought them closer, but Tate's amazing spirit and kind heart had sealed the deal. Adrian could see a future with him, and it had to be one where Tate could do what he loved. If that meant they stayed here at the camp, then Adrian would find a way to make it work.

"What do you want to do tonight?" Tate asked as they let themselves into the cabin after dinner. "I could take you into Bloomington if you're stir-crazy. Hit some bars or see a movie or something."

Tate stretched, and Adrian watched the play of muscles through his thin T-shirt. His mouth went dry.

"I choose the *or something*," he said, grinning deviously when Tate turned around and gave him a questioning look.

"Oh," Tate breathed, his gaze darkening.

Adrian hummed in agreement and crowded into Tate's space until he had him backed up against Tate's closed bedroom door. He stopped just short of kissing him, letting his lips hover a millimeter away from Tate's as their gazes locked. It was more intimate than anything Adrian had ever done. Standing with their breath mingling, Adrian felt like they were actually a part of each other. If the moonmate bond could make this innocent contact feel so intense, what would sex with Tate be like?

He wasn't going to wait any longer to find out. Adrian closed the tiny gap between them and kissed Tate, reveling in the way their lips fit together like they were made for each other. Tate responded eagerly, his hands fitting around Adrian's waist and ushering him closer.

Adrian shivered when Tate's thumbs stroked up under his T-shirt, the skin-on-skin contact a delicious preview of what was to come. He paused, worried for a moment that the shiver might be the start of a shift, but it wasn't. Just pure, unadulterated pleasure.

When Tate pushed up Adrian's shirt and slid his hand up his back and around to ghost along his side Adrian bucked against him, breaking the kiss with an undignified giggle.

Adrian buried his face in the warm skin of Tate's neck. "Sorry. Ticklish."

Tate resumed his exploration, his hand running up between Adrian's shoulder blades. "I want to get to know all of your quirks," he said, groaning when Adrian nuzzled in closer.

"Well, I have a thing for necks," Adrian said, nipping playfully at the thin skin. Tate shuddered, and a thrill shot through Adrian. His voice turned husky. "It looks like that's something we share."

He hissed out a surprised laugh when Tate turned the handle of the door and they stumbled inside. Tate guided him over to the bed, walking backward so he didn't have to disentangle them. He collapsed onto the bed, and Adrian scrambled to brace himself on his arms so he didn't crush Tate as he fell on top of him.

They bounced on the mattress, and the friction of his erection rubbing against Tate's made Adrian whimper.

"I have a thing for *you* and anything that makes you sound like that," Tate murmured. He canted his hips up, drawing a low moan from Adrian this time.

Adrian leaned down and kissed him, moving his hips against Tate's. The tightness of his jeans was enough to keep him from embarrassing himself, so he just enjoyed the sensation of being so close and drawing gasps and shivers from Tate underneath him.

"We are too old," Tate began, pausing to kiss Adrian again, "to come in our pants."

"Then we'd better get the pants off," Adrian said, working a hand between them to thumb at his button and zipper. The motion brought him into contact with Tate's straining erection, and he lost focus, curving his hand around the bulge and sinking back down to kiss Tate.

Tate drew in a breath. "I don't like our chances if you keep that up."

He shifted Adrian off him and lifted his hips to tug at his pants. Adrian rolled off the side of the bed, stood, and shimmied out of his jeans. His boxers were already smeared with precome, and he peeled them off before climbing back onto the bed and straddling a now-naked Tate.

Adrian hadn't thought to take off his shirt, but before he could grab the hem, Tate's hands were already there, lifting it over his head and tossing it onto the floor.

When Adrian leaned forward, their cocks brushed, and it was electric. Abandoning his plan to take things slow, Adrian got a hand around both of them and started to stroke. Tate sat up, cradling Adrian's head with one hand, and then rolled them so they were on their sides. It changed the angle of Adrian's strokes and left both of them breathless.

Tate's hand joined his, and they moved faster. The new position brought them close enough to kiss, and Adrian swallowed down sighs and moans greedily, his tongue licking into Tate's mouth in search of more.

Adrian tried to slow down when he felt his orgasm begin to build, but Tate sped up instead, and it didn't take much more before Adrian was falling over the edge, lost in a pleasure more intense than anything he'd ever felt before. His mouth fell away from Tate's and he rested his head on Tate's shoulder, his body spasming as the waves of his orgasm worked through him. Tate brought up a hand and rested it over the back of Adrian's neck, holding him close, Adrian's cries muffled against his skin.

After the last spasm, Adrian went boneless against Tate's firm chest, letting Tate take all of his weight. Tate pressed a kiss to the top of his head and shifted him to the mattress so he could raise up on his knees, his hand still working over his own cock furiously. Adrian reached out and cupped his balls, massaging them as Tate started to come. Tate fell forward, but Adrian was ready for him, recovered enough to support him as Tate came all over his chest.

Tate fell heavily back to the mattress when he was finished, his breathing ragged.

"Jesus Christ," he panted. "That was—"

Adrian laughed. "*That* was apparently moonmate sex."

"Sign me up," Tate said, still winded.

"It's definitely a perk. I think I could get used to being moonmates."

Tate groped around the mattress, grasping Adrian's hand when he found it. "Me too."

# *Chapter Twenty*

*One week later*

**IT** had been strange to sleep in a different bed from Adrian last night, but since they were bunked up with four other wolflings to ride out the full moon, that hadn't seemed appropriate.

Instead, Tate had spent the night in a narrow twin bed, catching snippets of sleep when he could while the wolflings played cards and horsed around all night. Adrian had joined in with them, and Tate had enjoyed watching him interact with the teens. He was a great mentor, and he'd be a fabulous addition to the staff if Anne Marie got her way and Adrian chose to stay.

Not that Tate was going to let that happen. Adrian was meant for a lot more than a sleepy werewolf camp tucked away in southern Indiana. They'd agreed to take each day as it came, and Adrian was planning to extend his stay at Camp H.O.W.L. through the next moon, commuting to his company's Indianapolis office once or twice a week to take care of any work he couldn't do from Tate's cabin.

Adrian wasn't the only one who'd been making plans, though. Ryan's father had been so grateful over Tate's role in his son's breakthrough that he'd offered to throw a frankly ridiculous amount of money at Tate to get Tate to relocate to New York and continue to see Ryan as a patient.

He and Adrian would need to talk it over, but not until he roused all the wolflings and got them back to their cabins.

"C'mon, bud," Tate said, nudging Ryan awake from his sprawl on the floor. "They're serving breakfast in the main room, and then you can finish packing."

Ryan grinned up at him blearily. "I didn't shift," he said, his words slurred with exhaustion from a night spent fighting the effects of the moon.

"You did good." Tate offered Ryan a hand and pulled him to his feet. "Everyone did. You're all going to get to go home today."

Arms wrapped around Tate from behind, and he relaxed into Adrian's sleep-rich scent. "Not all of us."

Ryan made a gagging noise. "You two are worse than my parents. It must be a moonmate thing. You're all disgustingly adorable."

"Your parents are moonmates?" That was news to Tate.

"Yup. Bonded and sickeningly in love," Ryan said, sounding fond rather than annoyed. "I think that might be why things have changed so much. They have a pretty intense bond, and even though he's the Alpha, Mom has a lot of say in Pack matters. After I talked to them last week about college and being a disappointment and everything, my brother said Mom lit into Dad like a stick of dynamite."

Tate had talked to both of them yesterday, and that was probably an accurate assessment.

"Mom's upset because she didn't realize how I was feeling. I mean, how could she, though? I never said anything."

"I hope you told her that," Tate said, pride filling him. Ryan's father wasn't the only one who had come a long way. Ryan had thrown himself into therapy and camp activities, and it showed. He wasn't the surly, disrespectful, unhappy kid he'd been. Things weren't perfect, and Ryan still had a lot to work through, but he was blossoming into the man Tate had caught glimpses of over the last two months.

"I did. I told her you'd say that was self-defeating talk and that we need to look ahead of us instead of behind us."

Adrian pressed a chaste kiss to Tate's neck and pulled away.

"Sounds like we might have a budding psychologist here," he said, rubbing his knuckles over Ryan's freshly buzzed head. He'd shaved off the floppy locks a few days ago, saying he'd always hated it but so had his father, so he'd kept it like that out of spite.

Everyone else had already sprinted for breakfast, so Tate herded Adrian and Ryan out into the basement's common area. Kenya and Diann had saved all three of them plates of eggs and sausage. Ryan grabbed his and continued on to a table full of wolflings. Tate and

Adrian sat down, Adrian in front of the plate with a steaming cup of coffee next to it. Adrian grabbed it and murmured ridiculous things to it as he brought it up to his mouth to take the first sip.

"Good morning, gentlemen," Kenya said, her eyes bright. "I trust the moon treated you well?"

"Everyone was able to hold off their shift. I'm a happy man," Tate said, reaching over to take a piece of buttered toast off Adrian's plate. He replaced it with his bagel before he'd fully processed what he was doing. Adrian hated buttered bread, so it had seemed like the natural thing to do.

Adrian caught his eye and winked, making Tate flush. Ryan wasn't wrong. They were sickeningly adorable.

Diann leaned in. "Are you sticking with us for another month, Adrian?"

Adrian's mouth was full, so Tate answered for him. "He's going to split time between being here and being up in Indy."

"Just until November?" Diann asked, giving Tate a pointed look.

He'd already given Anne Marie his notice. Whether or not he took Ryan's father up on his offer, Tate knew he and Adrian couldn't stay at Camp H.O.W.L. He'd told Kenya and Diann last night too.

"What's happening in November?" Adrian asked after he'd swallowed.

"That's something we need to decide," Tate said. He shot a dirty look at Diann, who shrugged, unrepentant. She and Kenya were used to being the ones to push Tate into uncomfortable territory when it came to communication and emotions, but he didn't need as much help these days.

"I figured we could go for a walk after the kids leave, maybe sort some things out."

None of the scenarios Tate had in mind involved the two of them splitting up. A month ago he wouldn't have been able to fathom how he could choose to entangle his life with someone else's, but a lot had changed in that month.

Too much, really. Tate would have thrown a bag full of clinical terms at anyone who came to him with a story like his and Adrian's, so it was hard for his mind to accept what his heart had embraced so—at the risk of sounding trite—whole-heartedly.

Change was hard, and it wouldn't happen overnight. But Adrian—God. That man was patience personified, and Tate got the feeling he'd wait forever if necessary.

It wasn't. Tate was finally able to say the word moonmate without grimacing, and it was all because Adrian had helped him see that what the two of them had together was nothing like the so-called moonmates his father took. He'd twisted the idea into something manipulative and wrong, just like he'd bastardized the idea of Pack with the way he treated everyone on the compound.

Adrian studied Tate for a moment and then shrugged and picked up the bagel. "Sounds good to me."

The exhaustion of Tate's sleepless night melted away as he looked at Adrian. Being trusted and loved like that was powerful. And he was going to do everything in his power to shower all of that back on Adrian too.

He'd grown up thinking moonmates were a sham, a cycle of abuse and manipulation. But he'd had it wrong. Moonmates *were* a closed loop. That much was true. But it was a loop of love and support, not abuse.

Tate wasn't sure where they'd end up. There were a lot of long, messy discussions in their future. But whatever that future was, they'd face it together.

# *Epilogue*

*Six months later*

**"THIS** is the fourth box labeled 'notebooks,'" Tate said, dumping the contents on the floor in what would be their living room once they were unpacked. "I think we might need to have an intervention."

Eliza trailed in behind him with a box marked kitchen. "It's probably porn. Adrian is old-school. Your boy likes magazines instead of the internet," she said over her shoulder as she passed through. "He used to mix them in with his drawing notebooks in his desk because he didn't realize we could smell them."

Tate gave the box a wary sniff, but didn't pick up anything other than the scent of cardboard and the sharp smell of permanent marker.

Adrian's brother Thomas snickered, poking his head around the armoire he was assembling in the corner. "Did he? Damn. I just figured he was really into whatever he was drawing," he said. "Should have known no one likes buildings that much."

"You're all hilarious," Adrian yelled from the bedroom. "Shut up and get back to work. The truck is due back by seven or I'll have to pay for another day."

"Mom's paying for it anyway," Thomas muttered, but he picked up his screwdriver and went back to work. Even though they were separated by an entire country, he didn't seem to want to piss off his Alpha.

Tate didn't blame him. Even without any of the Pack ties that forced obedience, he'd been hesitant to defy her himself when they'd met. Tate's refusal to join her Pack had caused a rift in their normally close family, but once she—and the rest of the Pack—had understood why, they'd been accommodating and accepting.

Tate wasn't built to be part of a Pack. He'd had his Pack loyalty beaten into him as a child, and he'd never put himself in that position again. Even for an Alpha as fair and nurturing as Adrian's mom.

And now he'd found a job where his Packless status was a boon. He'd been reluctant to take Alpha Connoll up on his offer to come to New York because he'd assumed he'd have to join the Pack, but the Alpha had been surprisingly understanding. He'd even helped Tate set up a private practice in the city, something that would never be possible without the local Alpha's permission. Sometimes he missed Camp H.O.W.L. like a physical ache, but Kenya had been right. It had been long past time for Tate to move on. It hadn't been easy. Change was scary, especially to a confirmed hermit like Tate. But it had been a good move—he'd only been

here a few months and he already had a great base of
clients. It felt good to know he was really making a
difference when he went in to work every day. And now
that Adrian was here, everything was perfect.

"Mom isn't paying for anything, asshole," Adrian
said, smacking his brother on the back of the head as he
walked by. "The company is."

"Same difference," Eliza called from the kitchen.

"Hardly," Adrian scoffed. He bent down to press a
kiss to the side of Tate's neck, distracting Tate from his job
of filling the bookcases Thomas had assembled earlier.
Tate breathed in the scent of him, warmth blossoming in
his chest. "I'm the one in charge of the New York office,
which technically means *I* am paying."

"Semantics." Eliza breezed back out of the kitchen.
"I'm going to go pick up some food. The truck's mostly
empty."

Alpha Connoll had sent over a group of wolflings,
Ryan included, to help them unload. They'd made
pretty quick work of all the furniture that had been
crammed into the truck Thomas and Eliza had driven
cross-country for their brother.

"Lazy," Adrian teased.

Eliza shook her head. "Alpha," she said, pointing
to her chest.

"That's just another way of saying bossy." Adrian
ducked when Eliza winged a throw pillow from the
couch at him. It hit Tate instead, and he grabbed it
before Adrian could throw it back. This wasn't his first
rodeo with the Rothschild siblings, and he wanted to at
least get the apartment set up before they wrecked it.

"Besides, you're not the Alpha yet. You're just
jealous because I got a big promotion and you're still
working under Mom."

Alpha Rothschild had been reluctant to let her son leave Portland, but when Adrian had made it clear he was following his moonmate across the country with or without her permission, she'd cleared the way for him to manage the New York office of Rothschild Architects. Being separated from his moonmate had been hard, but Tate had been busy setting up his practice and getting to know the local Pack. Adrian would be inducted as a member at the next full moon, and after spending the last few months with them, Tate could understand why joining a Pack was important to Adrian. His bond to Adrian was enough for him, but he didn't begrudge Adrian the comfort of having a Pack. He was just relieved Alpha Connoll wasn't offended that he didn't want to join himself.

"I'm getting pizza," Eliza said, blithely ignoring Adrian's barb. She held out her hand. "And since I'm sure you got a nice raise with that promotion, you're paying."

Adrian handed over his credit card with a grin. "Have them send a few pizzas over to the Alpha's compound too."

Alpha Connoll had generously offered them an apartment in the sprawling building he owned, but Tate wanted a little more separation between himself and the Pack. Tate had taken a room there while he'd waited for Adrian to move out east, but he didn't want to share space with anyone other than Adrian now. He wanted more privacy than a Pack compound could offer.

Eliza opened her mouth and then scowled. Adrian's eyes lit up.

"You were going to say I wasn't the boss of you, weren't you? But I am!" He was practically cackling. Tate felt amusement thrum through their bond, wrapped up in warmth and satisfaction. Adrian had been worried his family would resent him for moving, but here they were, helping him put together his new life with Tate. It was more than either of them had dared hope for.

Eliza huffed and flounced out of the apartment as Thomas, Adrian, and Tate roared with laughter. It felt good to simply be happy, to let himself enjoy a moment without worrying when the other shoe might drop. Tate might be stubborn, but he wasn't stupid. Once he realized what he'd found in Adrian, he'd given himself over to it wholeheartedly.

His father had hung over his entire life like a pall, and making the decision to step out into the light had been scary. But Kenya was right—he was more than his history. And he wasn't going to let his past cast a shadow over his future anymore.

Right now, he and Adrian were building a life in New York. But who knew what the future would bring? Maybe Adrian would want to go back to his Pack in Portland at some point. Maybe they'd hate living in the city and find some quiet little town to settle down in.

It didn't matter where they ended up, as long as they were together. Camp H.O.W.L. had been his refuge for a long time, but it was time to move on. For the first time in his life, Tate had a home. And it was a person, not a place.

# *Coming in December 2017*

REAMSPUN BEYOND

**Dreamspun Beyond #9**
**Fangs and Catnip** by Julia Talbot

A romance worth fighting for—tooth and claw.

Solitary vampire Fallon Underwood gets all the social interaction he needs being the silent partner at the Dead and Breakfast B&B high in the Colorado mountains. Change is hard for Fallon, so when his business partner Tanner suggests hiring a new manager for the inn, he's adamant that they don't need help, especially not in the form of bouncy werecat Carter Hughes.

Carter is a happy-go-lucky kitty, and he loves the hospitality industry, so the D&B ought to be a great place for him. He falls for Fallon as soon as he picks up one of Fallon's novels and begins to woo the vamp with gifts. When Fallon finally succumbs to Carter's feline charms, the results are unexpected to say the least. Their mating will have irreversible consequences—for their bodies and their hearts.

**Dreamspun Beyond #10**
**The Gryphon King's Consort** by Jenn Burke

Love takes flight.

The sudden death of the Gryphon King throws the kingdom of Mythos into uncertainty. Luca, the Crown Prince, rushes both his coronation and an arranged marriage to a man he's never met. Eirian is young and idealistic, and while both of them want what's best for their people, their philosophies couldn't be more opposite. While Luca believes in honoring tradition, Eirian is determined to infuse modern values into their kingdom of magical creatures. When given the choice between his crusade and loyalty to his husband, Eirian makes a decision that might ruin any hope of the marriage succeeding.

Still, Luca is committed to making their union work, and that means forgiving his brash consort. But when Eirian becomes the target of a conspiracy that puts his life in danger, Luca must act fast—or lose the chance to explore their burgeoning love forever.

# *Now Available*

## Dreamspun Beyond #5
**Dragon's Hoard** by M.A. Church

To be loved by a dragon is to be treasured.

A hundred years ago, werewolf Alpha Montgomery took a risk driven by desperation—he borrowed money from the ancient dragon Warwick Ehecatl, putting up the pack lands as collateral. Now the debt is due, and dragons don't forget—or forgive. Warwick demands Montgomery's son, Avery, and three businesses as compensation. As an Omega, Avery knows he is basically useless to his pack, so he might as well agree. He soon has second thoughts, though. Warwick is fearsome, and he's free to do as he likes with Avery.

Warwick knows his race's reputation, and he even admits some of it is deserved. But he'd rather cut off his tail than let his innocent mate's light go out. It won't be easy, but buried deep, there's something between them worth safeguarding.

## Dreamspun Beyond #6
**The Supers** by Sean Michael

Hunting ghosts and finding more than they bargained for.

Blaine Franks is a member of the paranormal research group the Supernatural Explorers. When the group loses their techie to a cross-country move, newly graduated Flynn Huntington gets the job. Flynn fits in with the guys right off the bat, but when it comes to him and Blaine, it's more than just getting along.

Things heat up between Blaine and Flynn as they explore their first haunted building, an abandoned hospital, together. Their relationship isn't all that progresses, though, and soon it seems that an odd bite on Blaine's neck has become much more.

Hitchhiking ghosts, a tragic love story forgotten by time, and the mystery of room 204 round out a romance where the things that go bump in the night are real.

*Love Always Finds a Way*

 REAMSPUN BEYOND

*Subscription Service*

*Love eBooks?*

Our monthly subscription service gives you two eBooks per month for one low price. Each month's titles will be automatically delivered to your Dreamspinner Bookshelf on their release dates.

*Prefer print?*

Receive two paperbacks per month! Both books ship on the 1st of the month, giving you *exclusive* early access! As a bonus, you'll receive both eBooks on their release dates!

Visit
***www.dreamspinnerpress.com***
for more info or to sign up now!

CPSIA information can be obtained
at www.ICGtesting.com
Printed in the USA
FFOW03n1551021117
41712FF